THE
DISCOVERY
OF SOCKET GREENY

TONY BERTAUSKI

ACKNOWLEDGMENTS

This project started several years ago as a story for my son, but it evolved into characters I just couldn't let die. There are so many people that have kept Socket Greeny on life support with professional help and encouragement.

My writing needed desperate help in the beginning and without the editorial efforts from Ellen Streiber, Meg Bertini, and Jeanine Le Ny, I'd still be toiling with paper-thin characters. I owe a great debt of gratitude to the folks at The Editorial Department for their professional assistance and camaraderie. Ross Browne, Jesse Steele, and Teresa Kennedy made me a better writer. And thanks to Jane Ryder for all those orange slices. It was fun.

On the home front, there have been countless friends and family that read numerous drafts that crept ever so slowly to a finished product. You have all been very kind to read my stuff. I know it wasn't always fun. Dylan Walsh was my only fan for quite some time and I often wrote just for him.

Most importantly, I have to thank the most significant person in my life. She's read every single draft and provided unparalleled support throughout the years. She's the one with the freckled complexion, the one with the red ponytail and the one that could always see through me. She's my lovely wife. Thanks, Heather.

Dedicated to those who search.

I

Virtualmode: an alternate reality where there is no pain.
No consequences. No fear. A place that is numb and safe.
Not cold, but empty.

NO RIME OR REASON

Your entire life can change in one day.

It's not like my life didn't need it. Basically, I lived a life of killing time. I was zoning out on a steady diet of video games and energy drinks. The only thing that made school even slightly bearable was getting into a fight at the end of the day. Sometimes, the sound of a nose crunching made life worth living. Even if it was my nose.

The day my life went inside-out started like any other day. I got to study hall just before the bell rang. Chute was reclined with her eyes closed and the transplanter discs behind her ears. Her red ponytail was hanging over the seat. Streeter had already crossed over. He was lying back with a grin on his face and his fingers laced over his belly.

I stuck the transplanters behind my ears. They sucked at the soft skin under my earlobes. My small hairs stood up and a spot quivered in my head like a tuning fork. The numbing took over.

There were no lights in the darkness behind my eyelids. No colors. A deadening sensation oozed down my neck and consumed me. Sound faded and the outside world drifted away. Temperature became non-existent. I left my skin behind and my awareness—whoever *I* am — was drawn into the Internet and transplanted into virtualmode.

For the moment, I drifted in darkness with the falling sensation. This was the place where most people failed to enter virtualmode. They couldn't handle the drifting. Virtualmoders knew how to ride the in-between like a wave.

I entered my sim that looked pretty much like my skin, except for the hair. I liked my sim bald. Back in the skin, my hair was past the shoulders and white as snow. Don't know why it didn't have color.

Darkness took form. First, there was an empty room with lumpy, colorless furniture. The gray walls turned into wood paneling with frosty windows. Cheap sofas, frayed rugs covered the floor and monstrous deer heads looked down from mounts, their glassy eyes reflecting the fire in the hearth. Above the fireplace was an enormous moose head.

The flames flickered over the dry wood, occasionally licking the old stone around it. The top of the mantel unfolded and a tiny woman, blond hair and sweeping curves, stepped out and crossed her perfectly smooth legs.

"Can't feel the heat?" she asked. "Upgrade your gear with Dr. Feelers' tactile attachments. Dr. Feelers puts you in control of the nervous system inputs, you can feel as little or as much as you like. Fire too hot? Turn it down by —"

"Off." Chute's sim was taller than her skin. It was leaner and more dangerous. "Dr. Feelers don't work," she

4

mumbled, even though she was rubbing her hands in front of the fire.

A giant barbarian came out of the next room with a wooden chair that looked tiny in his hand. Streeter's sim was ten feet tall, muscles bulging off his neck and rippling down his arms with a bloody axe dangling from his hip. I always thought he should just go the whole nine and wear a loincloth. Dude was four feet tall in the skin, the shortest high school sophomore who ever lived, but in virtualmode he was a god.

He kicked the sofa away to make room and sat in the chair that groaned and splintered but somehow held him. Control panels emerged from the floor and wrapped around him like mission control.

"What're we doing here?" I asked.

"We're going to get our kill on."

"I just got pardoned for fighting. We get caught, just stamp my suspension."

"Don't worry, Buxbee's out of town." Streeter's rich voice vibrated off the walls. "That substitute has no idea where we're going. I set up a false scenario. As far as anyone's concerned, we're reliving Desert Storm for history class."

I looked at Chute. "Did you know we were doing this?"

"He didn't tell me. If you were in class on time, he wouldn't have told you, either." She turned her head, the ponytail whipping around. "That's the way he does it."

"All right," Streeter sang to himself. "If you're wondering where we are, I hacked us into a world—"

"Whoa, wait a second." Chute held up her hand. Her sim looked like it had never seen the sun. "I don't think we need to be hacking into anything, Streeter. You got caught last time and we don't need to be wandering around some protected world *while we're in class!*"

His bushy eyebrows knitted together like enormous caterpillars. "First of all, I didn't get *caught* last time,

5

someone ratted me out. And they couldn't prove I hacked anything so, technically, I wasn't caught. Secondly, stop being a wuss. Right, Socket? Right?" He smacked me with a fist the size of a basketball. "We're in, we're out, no harm, no foul or whatever else jocks say before a game. We're not getting caught. Besides, this place is one hell of a ride. I hacked in the other night just for a little taste and me likey."

I didn't care one way or the other. I never wanted to admit it to Streeter, but I was getting a little bored of virtualmode battles. So was Chute, I could tell. But Streeter lived for it so I shrugged.

Streeter smiled. "All right, good. This place is called the Rime. It's a bunch of twelve-year olds with rich parents. I say we vaporize their asses down to bare data and harvest all their experience points. They aren't worth shit, but who says we can't have a little fun."

"Twelve-year olds?" Chute said. "Seriously?"

"Yeah, seriously. We ain't got time for a real battle. It's just a little quickie, come on."

The monitors lit up. Streeter scanned them, mumbling to himself as he surveyed the environment outside the cabin. Chute was already sitting on the couch with her arms locked over her chest checking her emails. She wasn't going to talk, so I figured I'd check mine, then changed my mind. There'd just be a thousand unread emails and I wasn't going to read them. Besides, there was likely a video message from Mom with the worn out face telling me she wouldn't be home tonight. Again. So I sat next to Chute and zoned out for a while.

"You all right?" Chute said.

"Yeah, I'm all right. You?"

"Something's bothering you."

Life was bothering me, but I couldn't explain that to her. It was just one of those days, but I could never hide it from Chute. She looked right through me.

Streeter clapped his hairy-knuckled hands that sounded like paddles and smiled, his teeth big and square and chipped. "Let's shred some twelve-year-old ass."

"Don't say it like that," Chute chimed.

Our clothes shifted and changed, turned white, speckled with browns and blacks and hung like rags. A battle staff appeared in Chute's hands. Evolvers materialized on my belt, simple handles that looked less threatening than Chute's pole but, once activated, transformed into any weapon I visualized.

A clean-cut kid appeared at the door. "Are your weapons weak? When you need to destroy and do it fast, think the Canonizer." He held up a pistol with an oversized barrel. "It's rapid, compact, and requires a fraction of the code—"

We walked through the apparition and his cheesy weapon onto the front porch. The boards were gray and weathered like the sky. The cabin was buried in a dense forest. A narrow path at the bottom of the steps carved between the snow-crusted trees. My breath came out in long clouds.

I could feel all the way back to my skin and it felt cold. Maybe it was my imagination or maybe I was just nervous. Or maybe things were about to get really weird.

SHADOWPLAY

My guts were everywhere.

I was staring at a gray sky streaked with snowflakes blowing like tiny bullets, remembering two words. *True Nature.* Someone whispered them into my ear just before something happened.

Everything seemed so unreal, like time was moving in slow motion. The sky was like a steel sheet that concealed the sun. It looked cold. There were shouts and the howling of wind but even that was blotted out by a high-pitched whine inside my head like I'd been knocked out with a concrete block.

Putty-like goo bubbled and burped from gaping holes in my chest and my stomach was just plain gone. Instead of intestines, the ground was splattered like someone dropped a brick in a bucket of paint.

Just my sim. For a second, I forgot I was in virtualmode, afraid that was my skin smeared on the ground. *Why am I still here? If I died in battle, I should've been kicked back to the skin. And why can't I remember anything?*

I was on a frozen tundra with snowy dunes rolling all the way to the horizon and pointed snow-capped mountains in the far off distance, but where I was laying it was bare ground like some sort of fiery meteorite filled with gray gooze exploded. There was a shadow in the white landscape, slipping among the scoured snow drifts like a tattered ghost fleeing the scene of a crime. Suddenly, a giant blocky-toothed barbarian was leaning over me, his face criss-crossed with pink scars. Streeter's lips were moving but I barely heard the words.

"Bail out! Code bail out!"

A girl slid across the ground and elbowed him out of the way. Somehow, her cowl stayed pulled over her head but her red hair spilled out. "Get us out of here, Streeter!"

"What'd you think I'm doing?"

"You're standing there with your thumb up your ass!" She cradled my head and bit her lip against the wind that was biting back. "I told you, Socket, I told you," she said, not so quiet, "I told you we shouldn't let him hack us in here. I told you something would go wrong." She held up her hand, my guts dripped off in the wind. "You knew it, too."

Maybe I did, but I always felt like something was wrong. With me. With the world. Everything.

Streeter was screaming and cursing. Something wasn't working. Bail out always took us back to the skin. "I told you, Streeter," Chute shouted, "now those Rimers got us locked in here until they shred our sims to goop! We'll be lucky if they don't report us to the cops!"

"Just shut up, let me think for a second!"

Streeter stomped around, muttering to himself, thinking out loud before falling on the ground and hunching over something in his hand.

"What happened?" My voice echoed in my head.

"We don't know," Chute answered. "Something exploded." She glanced down at my farting chest wounds. "We don't know how that happened."

The shadow ghost was back, playing peek-a-boo in the snow as it weaved in and out of the ground, its body flapping madly. I pointed at it now standing beside Streeter but Chute pushed my hand down. "Try not to move, it's only going to screw up your sim. It's going to take like a month to fix as it is." She bit her lip again but not against the wind, this was more about Streeter.

"That thing." I nodded at it. "Who is that?"

She looked. "What thing?"

"That shadow."

She looked again but only shook her head.

"He's delirious." Streeter was now sitting with his legs folded, poking at something in his hand.

"It's right there," I said, pointing again.

"Look, there's no shadow sim." He waved his hands right through it. *How could he not see it?*

"It's right next to you."

"You're brain damaged. Shadow sims can't stabilize in this environment, so just relax, I'll get us out of here."

"You better," Chute said.

"You're such a wuss," he replied.

"And you're dead meat if you get us suspended."

"Relax, we're not going to get caught by that lame-ass substitute, he doesn't know his bunghole from a hole in the ground. I guarantee he doesn't know how to monitor virtualmode activity. And the cops would be here already if the Rimers were going to report us, so just freaking relax, all right." He snorted, shaking his head, thinking *wuss.*

10

But they were missing the obvious. There was a shadow standing right in front of us and only I could see it. And now each time the shadow moved, I felt a tug somewhere *inside*, all the way back to my skin that was sitting in study hall.

Chute closed her eyes, shaking her head. I took her hand. She was probably reclined in the study hall with the same worried frown crunching the freckles between her eyebrows. I could almost feel her skin tense up. And then I realized I *could* feel it. I could feel her hand cupped inside mine. It was warm and shaky. And the bits of sleet and snow stung my cheeks. Each time I felt the tug of that shadow moving around, I could feel more, like I was a vessel filling up from the inside.

I should've been having a full-blown freak out. Feeling something in virtualmode? But I felt Chute's fingers scratch me as she lifted my head. I could smell the fragrance of her hair snapping in my face like fine whips.

"This is weird," I said. "I can feel you."

"What?" Chute put her ear closer to my lips.

"You guys want to stop playing boyfriend/girlfriend for like two seconds and help me?" Streeter said.

"I'm sorry," Chute shouted, "do you need some help? Here." She scooped up a handful of liquid guts and splattered it along Streeter's backside. "Anything else?"

He looked over his shoulder. "That really wasn't necessary."

While those two argued, I rubbed my fingertips together, feeling the brittle texture of my fingerprints and the arctic wind bite my exposed skin. My senses sharpened quickly, but it went beyond that. I felt the ground under my back and the snowflakes drive across the snow drifts, like I was becoming part of the environment, plugging into the ground. I sensed the surroundings like they were my own body and the cold was no longer cold and the wind no longer windy because I was the cold and I was the wind. I felt the shadow sweeping around me. It felt so familiar, like seeing someone I once knew.

I felt the ground tremble. Felt the bodies growing from the frozen soil beneath the blanket of snow before I actually saw them emerge like blackened sunflowers.

I yanked Chute's flapping sleeve and jerked my head in the direction of the disturbance. She looked over, sat up straighter. The wind knocked her hood off; her long hair whipped sideways. "We're screwed."

The sunflowers transformed into small, stout warrior thugs with beards and bushy eyebrows with battleaxes and long swords they gripped with sharpened claws. There were a hundred of them that slowly worked toward us through the snow. Seemed like the wrong sort of warrior sims to have in a world of snow drifts, but they'd get to us eventually.

Streeter leaped up and pulled his staff out of the snow. It was as thick as a tree trunk topped with spikes with bits of skin and hair and brains. He looked at the sky like he was studying the weather then bowed in prayer. An electrical field crackled around the spikes and dark clouds rolled out of the gray sky like smoke pushing through holes from the other side. I could feel my hair stand on end. Streeter rammed the staff on the ground and lightning bolted down, frying every one of the tiny warriors in their tracks, leaving behind smoldering holes.

"That's called a shit storm," he said.

"There's more coming," I said.

"Yeah, well I can't keep pulling lightning out of my ass, it takes too long to power up." He jerked his head at Chute. "Why don't you do something?"

"What do you want me to do?" Chute answered. "I'm a healer."

"Oh, yeah. I almost forgot." He stared at my dripping chest cavity and rolled his eyes. "You're doing great."

"That's it." She was on her feet reaching into her sleeve. Streeter held out his hands, not trembling or in surrender but begging her to rethink. Chute pulled a long, slender staff from her sleeve, impossibly long to fit inside her cloak, and spun too quickly for the barbarian to do anything. The pole flexed under the velocity of her swing and it cracked on the back of his legs, making a sound like a textbook dropping flat on a desk.

"Socket!" Streeter dropped on his knee. "You better stop her!"

"I'll show you how much I suck!" Chute dropped three more quick shots on him, deftly avoiding his half-hearted attempt to snatch her. She flipped over him and drove the staff into his back, driving him face first into the snow. "Who sucks now, douche bag!"

Streeter could've knocked her halfway across the tundra, if he wanted to. Sometimes he did, but most of the time he let her get it out of her system. Sometimes I broke it up and sometimes I watched their spats play out and they always ended with one of them damaging the other's sim and then cursing each other for all the trouble. This time, I didn't do anything because I was *feeling it*. I felt Chute's muscles tense, Streeter's knees throb. And this time I stopped them not by stepping between them. I stopped them with a thought.

[Stop.]

Chute was in mid-strike, ready to put a hole through Streeter's right lung, when the thought struck her and her body obeyed as if the thought was her own. She looked around, like someone had whispered it to her, but I simply willed her to step off Streeter. Streeter looked up, his scraggly beard powdered with snow. They could feel something, too. They could feel me inside them. And then they watched my stomach begin to rebuild itself, regenerating simulated flesh, filling the holes in my chest until my body was whole again.

Streeter got on his knees and looked at Chute. "I owe you an apology."

"I didn't do anything." Her mouth barely moved. "How'd you do that?"

The shadow walked up behind her and through her and stood between us, its ghostly form snapping in the wind. I sat up and looked at my hands, unsure if this was virtualmode or a dream.

"Do I know you?" I asked the shadow.

Streeter and Chute looked at each other. Streeter said, "I think he's having a stroke."

"Socket, are you all right?" Chute asked.

But I didn't hear her words. I felt them, understood them like they were my own. I penetrated everything in this world, felt the tree limbs blowing on the mountaintops and the squatty warriors emerging in the distance again. I was everything except the shadow. I got up without much effort, like I levitated onto my feet.

[You've known me your entire existence.] The thought was in my head, but it was not mine. It came from the shadow that had no face.

"Did you do this to me?" I raised my hand, rubbing my fingertips. "Are you making this happen?"

"You're starting to worry me." Chute stepped through the shadow and stopped so the two were superimposed, making her fair complexion a shade darker. "We need to get you back to the skin."

"Yeah, get off the crazy train, Socket," Streeter huffed, gripping the staff with both hands. "I'm going to need some help for the next wave."

"Who are you?" I asked.

The shadow didn't gesture, shrug or say anything. It remained superimposed over Chute's worried expression. Whatever she said after that was lost in the wind. The familiarity of the shadow had a taste and a smell, some sort

14

of presence not generally associated with one of the five senses. I felt it like a thought or an intuition.

"Did you heal me?" I asked.

[You were never broken.]

"Socket, you're freaking me out, here," Chute said.

"I ain't got time to wait for him to come back." Streeter charged past me and my crazy rambling. The tiny Nordic warriors were black as tar, staining the snow as they shoved through the drifts. They were close enough to hear their snarling. Streeter let out a war cry, the same one he let loose before every clash, the same howl that Chute said made him look like a drama queen, and charged ahead to meet them head-on, bringing down the spiked club to crush the first one's skull.

Something squirmed in my belly. I had the vision of a bright star twinkling inside my stomach. A spark that, for a moment, blinded me. I felt my mind wrap around it and fuse with it.

And then things slowed.

Things stopped.

I could see in 360-degrees as if every particle of snow that hung sparkling in mid-air like tiny Christmas ornaments were my eyes. I did that. I was the one that willed the world to stop, for the wind to die and everything in it to take a timeout while I could think. I didn't intend for things to actually stop, but that's what I wanted and that's what happened. I took one of the snowflakes between my finger and thumb, studying the crystalline detail. It began to melt and water dripped down to my knuckle.

It was dead silent. Dead still.

The shadow was standing in front of Chute. Without the wind, his form shimmered like smoky particles loosely clinging together. I opened my mouth trying to figure out what the familiar flavor was, trying to figure out just who the shadow was. And then a thought came from somewhere deep inside, some place that had been stored in the lockers of a three-year old toddler. I was in a bathroom and smelled the scent of a man shaving at the sink. It was a safe smell. The man rinsed the razor and smiled down at me.

I couldn't bring himself to say it, couldn't say the word that I identified with this essence I was experiencing because the man that was shaving was dead. He died when I was five.

"What the hell is going on? Is this some sort of goof?"

I reached for the shadow but my hand waved through the wispy form and as it did the essence tasted stronger, tingling all the way to my stomach, wrenching me with a helpless sense of falling, almost dropping me to my knees. But the essence was unmistakable. *Father.*

[The time has come to know who you are.] The thought had a distinct tone, but it was unlike the voice I remembered as my father's. *[For you to know your true nature.]*

Time wasn't to be measured in that still moment. The hands on a clock would not be moving. At some point, I stepped forward and merged with the shadow and the essence filled my emptiness, those pockets I did not know existed. Emptiness that yawned inside and sometimes pissed me off, made me sad and pissed me off at being sad. Emptiness for my dad dying and emptiness that he left me to figure things out on my own. Emptiness for having to look at the emptiness in my mother's eyes. Emptiness that left me awake at night staring at the ceiling wondering what the hell was the point of living. And now I didn't feel those things. I felt so present. So complete.

When the ground trembled, I realized I'd closed my eyes. The shadow was no longer there. And the ground continued to shake. The snow vibrated and the statue-like sims of Chute and Streeter shook, too. I no long felt connected with them or the rest of the environment.

On the horizon, the ground broke open and snow spilled inside a widening crevasse that snaked towards me, ripping

16

the ground like God had grabbed both ends of the world and decided to pull it apart. I watched the rip race under my feet. The falling sensation was back in my stomach because this time I was falling for real, down into the empty blackness that tasted like essence, that sixth sense, only this time it tasted steely and hard.

Blackness was all there was. No sim. Just falling.

I felt the hot needles of my sweaty skin sticking to the armrests of the study hall chair. I opened my eyes back in my skin. A silver ball hovered in front of me. Its surface gleamed like polished metal with a red eyelight beneath the surface. "The three of you must follow," the lookit said.

I was firmly planted in the seat, but still felt the falling.

PERP ALLEY

"Justin Heyward Street," the lookit announced.

"You know, middle names are so unnecessary," Streeter said, sitting forward and rubbing the feeling back into his face.

"Anna Nancy Shuester," the same lookit announced. Chute quickly did the same as Streeter.

"Socket Pablo Greeny." Its red eyelight shot right into my eyes. "The three of you are to follow."

Honestly, I still wasn't sure where I was. I gripped the armrest like my chair had been dropped from a cargo plane. I was still trying to return to my skin. I felt out of sorts, like half of my awareness was somewhere else. Back in my sim?

The lookit wasn't going to wait. It was about to call security when the room suddenly erupted. All the virtualmoders sat up, groaning and cursing, ripping the discs from behind their ears. The lookit's eyelight was spinning, recording the hundreds of study hall sound infractions. It blazed around the room trying to get control, then called for security and returned to the front row. The substitute teacher was watching a music video, looked up and closed his laptop.

"The three of you must follow," the lookit repeated.

I could barely feel my legs when I sat forward. Chute hooked her finger around mine and led me up the steps like the living dead. The queens, rats, burners, gearheads, jocks and goths and anyone else that couldn't thought-project into virtualmode looked up from their laptops and tablets and stared at us. Virtualmoders were all back in their skin.

"Did you do this, Streeter?" someone shouted. "Did you crash virtualmode?"

"Psssht. Noooo." He wasn't guilty, not this time. Streeter walked faster as wads of paper came flying.

Perp Alley consisted of five plastic chairs against the wall. A heavy door with wire-imbedded glass was across from the plastic chairs and behind that were the offices of the Dean of Boys, the Dean of Girls, various assistant principals, and the principal. This trip had the Dean of Boys stamped all over it.

I was feeling better after walking down the hall. The lookits wouldn't let us talk and that was all right, it gave me some time to think. Streeter had already asked what the hell happened. *What happened? I was haunted by a ghost, that's all. Oh, did I mention it was my dead dad? Yeah. Oh, and I stopped time and connected with the entire universe and experienced a moment of spiritual oneness. Any questions?*

Once we sat, I told them about the shadow, that time seemed to stop and the world split open, that it must've been some special weapon the Rimers set off, and blah,

blah, blah, I don't know what happened, either. Crazy shit happens all the time in virtualmode.

"The world split open?" Streeter asked. I described the black crevasse. "That's serious, Socket. I mean, if you fell inside that rip you could be disembodied, your awareness floating somewhere in the in-between forever and ever. They did a special on Discovery, virtualmoders that lay there like vegetables for months and months after they got swallowed in a crash."

I didn't bother telling him I did fall in.

Chute was looking more through me, sort of like a cop looking for the truth. I buried my face in my hands when the room started spinning. I wasn't falling, but both my feet weren't exactly on the ground. Chute rubbed my back. I just wanted off the ride.

"I want revenge," Streeter said.

"Just stop," Chute snapped. "We hacked into their world and they taught us a lesson and that's the end of it. Besides, you said it yourself, we crashed the world so it probably doesn't even exist anymore. You should be worried they'll find us and make us pay for it."

"Naw, they'll have safeguards against a hiccup like that, it'll snap right back together. Besides, those shitheads aren't going to report us because they were duping. Those little black things were automated versions of a dupe to avoid detection, like empty manikins with a single mission. They probably blew up Socket. Hell, we could report *them* to the cops and have *them* arrested for duping. But that wouldn't be any fun. I'd rather make them pay."

"They can dupe if they want to, it's a private world."

"Um, hello. Duplicating is illegal, in any form or fashion, read your virtualmode code laws: Any attempt to duplicate your identity, whether for business, recreation or just plain whatever, is not allowed under any circumstances. Period, the end. You know it, I know it. I

20

don't give a shit if they did it in their dreams. You can't dupe."

"I really don't give two craps," Chute said. "Why would anyone care what they do in their world? Stupid."

He walked several steps away, scratching his thick shag of brown curls like he needed a timeout from stupidity. When he returned, he had the intense look of concentration that flattened his face, made him look more like a frog than usual. He said slowly, "You don't listen in class, do you. First of all, I'm just going to ignore the improvement in safety that virtualmode laws have done, just forget all that. The world is going digital, Chute. In five years, half the world's population will be able to virtualmode, creating a digital reality with digital bodies and digital homes and everything, get it? People will be doing business from their homes, commerce and manufacturing and colleges will all be in virtualmode. If people start duplicating their identities, how the hell are you going to know what's real and what's not? You won't! So you can't dupe, Chute. Get it? You want to write that down so you don't forget? No. Duping. Period."

Chute jumped out of her seat and shook her finger right in his face. "Don't do that tone with me. I don't live and breathe for the virtualmode like you, so I don't know the stupid laws. Next time you talk like that, I'm stuffing you in a locker."

Streeter surrendered. "Hey, don't take your sexual frustrations out on me. I didn't blow Socket's mind." He snapped his fingers. "Socket, come back from the dead, buddy. Anytime now."

I looked at Streeter snapping. I shook my head, returning from a dreamy state. *I'm back in the skin,* I had to remind myself. Maybe Streeter was right. There were already studies suggesting that excessive virtualmoding was causing a disconnect between mind and body, where one would have a hard time distinguishing between reality and fantasy.

I needed a three-day suspension. Maybe stay off virtualmode the whole time. Streeter would bitch, but I needed a break.

Flip-flops slapped from around the corner and a girl with short, black hair flip-flopped in our direction. Streeter stared up at her with his tongue about to roll out. She had to walk around him, flicked her eyes at Chute rubbing my back and went into the administrative office, but not before a sudden drop in altitude pulled my stomach through the floor. I hung onto the chair for dear life.

[Socket Greeny, in trouble again? Shocker.]

"Did you hear that?" I said. "Did you hear what she was thinking?"

Chute clenched my arm tighter. Streeter and Chute looked at each other, exchanged knowing glances, then he sat on the other side of me. "Dude, you sure you're all right? I mean, you're starting to scare me a little with the wacky talk. You sure your nojakk isn't flaring up." Streeter tapped his cheek. "You hear me now? Hear me now?"

My cheek vibrated and I heard him through the nojakk seed imbedded in my cheek. But I heard the girl thinking. A thought was a thought, not a goddamn voice chiming from a nojakk. I waved him off and buried my face in my hands, again.

"Listen, buddy." Streeter dropped his hand on my shoulder. "You're not hearing voices or thoughts or stopping time. You're just in a fuzzy area, right now, reconnecting with the skin. It happens all the time, don't press it. Take some deep breaths, in with the good air, out with the bad." Streeter demonstrated deep breathing. "Don't crack on me. I need you."

"You're not taking him back to the Rime," Chute said.

"Don't be hasty. And you're not his mom."

22

I did take some deep breaths and did feel better. This was like a bad dream that took longer than usual to fade. The office door opened. The secretary stuck her head out. "All right, ya'll. Mr. Carter wants to see you now."

We got up. I felt fine but suddenly realized I was mad-crazy starving. I could feel my ribs poking through my shirt, like I hadn't eaten in days. Maybe I was getting a bit hypoglycemic. There was a girl in my social studies class that was hypoglycemic and she had symptoms like that. Maybe she forgot to mention the hallucinations. And thought-reading.

"Not you, Socket," she said. "Your mother will pick you up at the curb in a few minutes. You need to go right out."

"My mom?"

"She called right after ya'll got caught doing whatever you were doing and said you have a family emergency. Don't worry, you're still going to be suspended."

"Oh, man." Streeter stepped away from me like he might get infected.

I watched the two get escorted inside and past the secretary's desk. Chute turned and pointed at her cheek, mouthed the words *call me.* Streeter and Chute wouldn't be feeling too bad about their fate. Streeter lived with his grandparents and he would make up a story as to why he was home and they would believe it. Chute's dad would be upset, but he was always easy on her. But my mom?

Shit storm.

IN THE MOODY

Mom pulled into the parking lot. Her car was a silver, square thing. It didn't look like any model I'd seen on the road, certainly not one Ford or Chevy manufactured. It came from work, and like most things concerning her employer, I was clueless.

She was looking at the soccer field where a bunch of students were testing hovering jetter discs. Some new company donated them to the school, said the jetter boards had anti-gravity boosters that could carry 300 pounds and they wanted the virtualmoder students to learn how to ride them. They said they were sponsoring a new game that would revolutionize sports. Tacket or tagghet or something like that. Ordinarily, that would get my interest but anything that had to do with school and/or school spirit was immediately off my to-do list.

When I got in the car, she handed me two breakfast bars in white wrappers. "How'd you know I was hungry?"

She didn't answer, just eased through the parking lot. I tore open the first one and nearly swallowed it without chewing. My mouth filled with saliva and my stomach roared. It was like a shot of adrenaline tingling under my scalp. I chewed the second bar and lay my head back. Finally, I felt back to my skin. *What the hell are in these things?* The wrapper had no writing on it, no label, and no ingredients. I licked the inside of it.

We were on the Interstate heading towards Charleston. Mom gripped the wheel like it offended her. The skin over her knuckles pulsed. But she grabbed everything that way: coffee mugs, doorknobs, and little soft, innocent puppies. She stared blankly through the windshield. Maybe I was in trouble, I wouldn't really know for a while. We didn't talk about things that involved feeling.

That's the Greeny way.

I tapped up music on my nojakk and watched the traffic.

Half an hour later, we started over the 2.5-mile, cable-stayed bridge that crossed over the Cooper River. "We going shopping or something?" I asked.

She readjusted the stranglehold. "I'm taking you by the office."

"Awesome," I muttered. I didn't want her to hear that, but it was so silent in that car you could hear a sand flea fart. But she didn't take the bait, just kept her eyes ahead with one hand on the wheel and the other tucked under her arm. She was hiding her right hand.

"Thought you quit that," I said.

"Nothing wrong with a moody," she answered.

She fidgeted in her seat, then calmly put the moody cube in her purse and drank from a bottle of water. Her thumb was red and swollen. I knew about moody cubes, heard the warnings in school every day. Some company convinced the FDA that a little black square could stimulate dopamine production by relaying messages through the nervous system and relieve symptoms of depression and anxiety. They argued that because the brain was essentially a poppy field producing *natural* happy sedatives, it was nothing like narcotics. The FDA said sure, but it should at least be prescribed and the company responded, *Yeah, we're okay with that.*

I sometimes pressed her into giving up the habit because that couldn't be good. But sometimes I couldn't stand that dead-zone look on her face and just let her get some relief. I looked back out the window and watched the ships below, wishing I could smell the water or the salty South Carolina breeze but there was nothing getting inside that car. It's like we were sealed inside a tomb.

Mom drove through downtown, waiting more often for College of Charleston students and tourists then actual traffic. We passed the art dealers and law offices and souvenir vendors and old retired horses pulling antique-looking carriages full of New Yorkers and Mid-westerners listening to the driver, sitting backwards on the front, telling ghost stories and rehearsed jokes about the good old South and the charm of the Holy City.

Her office was a block past the regal steps of the Custom's House. It was just a simple black door wedged between an art gallery and a chocolate shop. No sign hanging on a rod perpendicular to the building or a window to see inside, just small letters on the door. *Paladin Nation, Inc.*

They were in desperate need of an advertising agency; they were barely a step up from a manhole. In fact, if you didn't look right at the door, you didn't notice it. I walked past it three times once. Mom slowed up to the curb just as a man stepped out of the door. A young guy in good shape with a proper haircut opened the car door for her. He didn't bother with me.

Mom waited at the office door. She pushed her hair behind her ear, it fell back, and took a deeper breath than usual. I thought she was more distant that usual. In fact, she felt cold. No, she *tasted* cold, like some sort of essence. I shook it off. Don't want to go there. I'd been grounded in my skin for a whole hour and preferred it that way. But I couldn't help noticing her coldness brought a taste of sadness with it. Sometimes I didn't even feel related to her, like she was just a stranger watching over me, like I was some sort of orphan. *Good times.*

The door led up creaky steps to a tiny room. There was a receptionist area behind a counter with a computer, desk, and files but there was never anyone there.

Mom told me to wait for her, she'd be right out, then went through the only door to the left of the receptionist area. I never went beyond that door. I had a vague memory of going beyond once with my dad when I was real little, but there wasn't much but a short hallway with three doors. The only thing I remember after that is a blue light and then I fell asleep, dreaming of caves and jungles.

I sat in the waiting room and slouched down. No magazine rack, no television or pictures of beaches with birds. I crossed my arms and laid my head back and closed my eyes but the slightest motion in my stomach made me bolt upright. Not going there. Nope.

I slid my fingers over the black iHolo strap around my wrist. An image illuminated above the strap like a holographic screen no matter which way I turned my wrist. I pushed the icons around, looked at a playlist I'd put together earlier that week and uploaded it to the nojakk, then booted up the music. While an acoustic guitar echoed inside my head, I went to my email and noticed the news headline.

International Virtualmode Blackout.

The story began in a virtualmode network hub inside a warehouse with a single isle going between lines of blue, pulsing orbs, five feet in diameter, encased in clear boxes with lab technicians wearing white coats and hardhats inspecting them. I'd seen portals before, the school had one in a basement below the Pit. It was the powercell that transported a user's awareness into virtualmode. I'd heard physicists explain how the intense power and density of portals allowed them to transcend time and space and interact simultaneously. Trippy shit. But no one cared how they worked, just that they worked.

"Sometime around 10:43, eastern standard, virtualmode experienced its first blackout," a reporter's voice announced as the lab technicians observed the portals. I turned the music down and sat up. "According to sources, a surge from somewhere in the world caused an international crash of all virtualmode worlds. Authorities say the balance of power has been restored and that normal activity has resumed, although there seems to be some confusion as to where the surge originated."

That's when the rip occurred. Did I make the whole thing crash? *Impossible.* Those portals were like a thousand nuclear reactors doing some sort of cold fusion. How in the hell—

Zzzzzsthhhp.

The iHolo image scattered for a second.

I shut down the music; felt the floor shutter. It came from the door. I was remembering the blue light again when the door opened and Mom was followed by a man. She stood to the side and let him pass. I jumped up.

The man walked fluidly. He was a bit older than Mom. His hair was streaked with gray and his face clean-shaven, what most women would call a handsome man with a smoldering attraction. He stopped only a few feet away, but the room was so small he couldn't get much farther away. I

28

wondered if I should bolt for the stairwell just in case a mugging was about to go down.

But then I *tasted* a taste, an essence. It was deep and sort of minty. Potent. I'd experienced that before. Maybe seen this guy before. Behind the door?

I looked at Mom. Christ, no one was saying anything. This was beyond awkward. The man was looking through me, studying me, like a doctor without the stethoscope and white coat. If he asked me to take my shirt off it was going to be stairway city.

"It's a pleasure to meet you, Socket." He extended his hand. I shook it. "Now that you're grown up."

I nodded, wondering why it felt like I was meeting the President.

"My name is Walter Diggs."

"Nice to meet you."

"It's been awhile since I saw you last, but I'm sure you don't remember. You were only that big." He put his hand down, the universal sign of a short person.

I was struggling with the memory of going through the door when I was *that big* and linking it to the minty essence, but the memory ended up in the caves and jungles. Then I remembered colored bats coming out of the trees. A real messed up dream.

"I knew your father," Walter said. "He was a fine man, he was. I was damn proud to have known him. No one could replace someone like Trey Greeny."

Oh, shit. Is this the stepfather talk? I'm not trying to replace your father, Socket, no one could. But I'm in love with your mother and you're going to have a new baby brother. Now go clean your room, asshole.

Walter started laughing. He looked over at Mom who returned his laughter with just barely a flicker of the corner of her mouth. He looked back at me. It was getting weird.

29

"What I'm trying to say is if you're half the person your father was, you'll have a lot to offer the world. But I suspect you're twice that."

"Thank you, Mr. Diggs, but I'm not sure what any of this means."

"Things are a little sketchy, I know. But it'll make sense real soon. Your mother is going to take you to meet some people in our facilities."

"I don't even know what you do." I shuffled back until my leg hit the chair.

"You will, soon." *Wink.*

No one winks when something really shitty is about to happen. Right? "Should I be worried right about now?" I looked at Mom. She was still cold. Walter offered a smile that, compared to Mom's, was like the sun.

"I can't tell you how happy I am to see you grown up. I look forward to working with you." He squeezed my shoulder, made eye-contact with Mom, and then was through the door from where he came, closing it behind him.

Mom opened the door to the stairs.

"Wait, what just happened?"

"There's a lot to explain," Mom said. She was itching for that moody. "I'll tell you everything on the way."

"We're not going with him?" I asked.

"The facility is a long way from here," she said. "But it won't take long to get there."

"We're flying?"

"No."

Now what in the hell does that mean?

WORMHOLED

The parking attendant was waiting out front with the door open. Mom took the first left turn and then another left down a narrow alley wedged between tall buildings. No one would notice it from the street, and if they saw it, wouldn't think to drive a car down it. It ended at a brick wall and backing out would seem impossible without swiping a door handle. There was a garage door on the left, which would've been directly below the office.

I had a feeling we were going wherever minty-man Walter Diggs went, although getting back in the car for a trip around the block made no sense. Mom had a whole life of secrecy. When she wasn't home, I'd go through her files, look under her mattress and through her closet to find out what she was doing. Now the gig was up and I was minutes away from everything. I always thought it would be more fun to find out.

The garage door opened and she eased into the lightless space as the door closed behind us. "This is going to feel funny," she said.

"You mean funny, ha-ha?" I answered. I was starting to squirm. The falling feeling was coming back.

"We're going through a wormhole, like a puncture in the fabric of time and space."

"Where we going?" I said, almost casually. Why not? Today wasn't making any sense, why not finish it with a trip through a rip in time. And space.

Mom laughed, sort of. It was mostly a hiccup, but not a smile, and certainly no joy.

A door in front of us began to open, blue light spilling out. "Close your eyes," she said. "And make sure your tongue is pushed against the roof of your mouth."

The blue light engulfed me. I clenched my eyes shut, grabbing onto the door. I felt like one of those cartoons getting steamrolled flat as paper. Thought I was going to scream, then puke. I didn't see blue. I didn't see anything. My lungs were burning and I gulped for air, drooling on my shirt when I realized we were through.

"Oh, Jesus," I blurted.

It was night. We were still in the car, although it wasn't moving. Instead, we were idling on a flat piece of ground with miles of boulder-strewn wasteland ahead of us without a road in sight. At the far end was a sheer-faced cliff. The full moon revealed streaks of ochre like ancient blood stains. It stood like a monolith, like God had plopped down a massive block of granite and said, "End of the world, assholes."

"This society has existed for as long as history's been recorded." Mom took a breath and touched the center panel. Lights appeared on the speedometer, holographic images illuminated the dash with maps and data and green dots and red dots and bullshit that looked more like a fighter jet than car. "We protect humankind from extinction."

"From what?"

"Once upon a time, it was natural disaster and plague and wars. In this era, the threat of extinction comes from humans." Her eyes appeared deeper-set in the moonlight and the glow of the instruments. "Humankind lacks understanding. As a species, we are still in our infancy. Out potential is limitless, but first we must survive to realize it."

"Are you one of them?"

"In a way."

"What's that mean?"

"It means the answer is complicated. There's a lot to understand, you'll have to be patient. For now, just know that we can do things that normal people can't."

She touched the control panel. Something thumped beneath the car. And then we were moving forward, only we weren't rolling. We were hovering. The car was flying. Not fast like spaceship fast, it was more like a slow hover that crossed over the impossible terrain. The wheels had folded beneath the car. No one was getting across this ground without one of these.

"You got to be shitting me."

"Watch your language, Socket."

I sat back, realized I was still holding onto the door. We were halfway to the red cliff when I relaxed. "What's this place called?" I asked. "This club, or society."

"The Paladin Nation."

"This is it, here?" I pointed at the looming cliff.

"No, it's all over the world. This is just one of the compounds."

I watched the cliff get closer. "We're not in South Carolina anymore."

She almost smiled, I could feel it.

There was no door in the side of the mountain. Instead, we passed through it, like it was only an apparition, into an enormous cavern. Mom touched a few buttons on the console and the car gently sank to the ground.

The cavern was dome-shaped, complete with authentic dripping stalactites. *Caves and jungles? Maybe that wasn't a dream.*

Mom pushed the steering wheel up and locked it out of the way. She gathered items from the backseat. I still hadn't let go. I had just taken my first ride in a flying car, hit a transportation wormhole, and now I was parked inside a mountain somewhere in the world that had mountains.

A large, gray sphere emerged from the wall. Several more appeared, floating inches above the ground like supersized lookits. They took position around the car, waiting.

"Servys," Mom said. "Technology is a bit more advanced here. You're going to see some things that don't exist in the outside world yet." She had her thumb buried in the moody, again. A look of eerie relief was on her face.

"I wish you'd stop that."

She closed her eyes, pushed her thumb in deeper. "There's so much to do, Socket. I just need to catch my breath."

"You don't have to save the world."

She tucked her hair behind her ear with her free hand. "Sometimes the world needs you and you have to be there. You'll understand one day. And I hope you find more strength than your mother."

I gently pulled her thumb from the moody, red and swollen. "You're plenty strong."

"Let's hope so."

She opened her door and stepped out. I turned to mine —a silver man was at the window. He had no face.

FACELESS

His egg-shaped head was featureless. No eyes or nose, mouth, ears or chin. Just a smooth, egghead with an eyelight pointed at me.

"Welcome to the Garrison, Master Socket." He waved a silver hand. "Do you need help exiting the vehicle?"

If I didn't see the colors move on his face, I would've sworn a real person said it. He looked like he was from a movie, standing six feet tall on two legs: A humanoid mech. The arms and legs were sinewy like an Olympian. And to top things off, he wore a loose plum-colored overcoat, sleeveless, cinched at the waist. But sure, why not. This was already shaping up like a dream, why not send in the flying dragons.

Mom was out of the car, explaining something to him. The servys repositioned themselves around her. One went to the back of the car, returned with her briefcase firmly gripped by an arm that had grown from its spherical body. The robe-wearing silver mech pointed at me. I was still grabbing the door. So far I'd looked at everything through the safety of a window. Getting out was another level. I reluctantly opened the door.

I've been here before.

It was the smell. Pleasantly musty and wet. Ancient. I was here long, long ago. Maybe it was take-your-kid-to-work day. I always thought it was a dream. Same cave, same smell.

"Socket," Mom said. "This is Spindle." The silver mech placed his hand on his belly and gestured with a small bow. "He's my assistant. He'll be your guide for the day."

"You're leaving?"

"I have to attend an urgent meeting." She touched my arm, like an apology. "Afterward, we'll meet in my office."

"Are you kidding me? You're just going to leave me here with... with..." Spindle's eyelight stared at me. "You can't do this to me, Mom. This isn't right. I've got crazy things in my head and you're flying a car and then there's the wormhole." I paced around, thought about taking a hit from her moody. "This is bullshit."

"Don't curse." Her left eye ticked. "We'll discuss it later. In the meantime, Spindle will escort you to security assignment. You're going to like him. You'll be safe."

Oh, great. Telling me I'll be safe meant I was in danger, like when someone says they ain't scared means they're really scared shitless. But Mom wasn't prone to signs of affection. It didn't happen often, so I was caught by surprise when she gently placed her hand on my cheek. "I'll see you in a couple hours."

[It'll be all right.]

That's what she was thinking. Instead of telling me where I was and why, she just wanted me to know it was all going to be all right. The last time she said that, she took me to the doctor for shots. While I waited, the nurse told me we were waiting on *a little stick,* then rammed a needle in my ass. I would've preferred a better explanation, then and now, but her touch and smile seemed to be enough for the moment. What else was I going to do? I didn't know how to fly that car and even if I did, where the hell was I going?

Mom was off to the only door in the cavern. The door slid open and closed behind her, leaving me with the muscular android.

"Do you have any questions?" Spindle asked.

His posture was friendly, his face bubbly yellow and orange. He was completely unaware I had just been squeezed through time and space for the first time like a birthing canal. But he waited patiently, the eyelight glowing, like a video game character waiting for my response.

"Okay. Ummm... where I am?"

"You are in the Garrison. It is one of many global training grounds of the Paladin Nation."

"Right. The Paladin Nation." I glanced around the cave. "Why haven't I heard about this place until about three minutes ago?"

"There are many things you have not heard of." He gestured to the servys still bobbing around us. "Nano-plastine technology, for instance. These servys are composed of cellular-sized nanomechs that make up a generic round body, much like the cells of your body. A processor is located at the core and can shift the cellular nanomechs into whatever form is necessary. Very useful. Humanity has not been granted access to this technology yet."

"What, you don't like to share?"

"Many discoveries are still considered too dangerous. When the circumstances are right, they will be released."

"These Paladins," I said, "they're human?"

"That is correct."

"What gives them the right to horde all this stuff?"

"The Paladin Nation is a much more evolved race of humans. The general public cannot be trusted with such power. It would be like giving a gun to a two–year-old child. In the hands of a responsible adult, a gun can be used safely. However, a two-year-old child would likely harm himself." He pushed his shoulders back and tilted his head. "Does that make sense?"

"But adults still shoot each other, so I'm not sure the gun analogy works."

"That is why it is a perfect analogy. Even guns are used irresponsibly. Can you imagine what the same people would do with some of these magnificent advancements?"

Spindle waited for my response. His facial colors were muted yellow, fading back to silver. He turned to the servys. His face jumped with dark blues but he said nothing out loud. The servys drifted back to the walls and merged through them as if the openings were all there, just masked with the illusion of rocky walls.

"If you have no more questions, we can proceed to security assignment. We can begin our journey with a friendly gesture." He held up his hand, fingers spread. "Stick it, Master Socket."

I looked at his expectant hand. "Do what?"

"Stick it." He shook his hand. "It is a friendly handshake that kids do. You stick it."

I held up my hand like his, expecting something like a high-five.

"No, no, you stick your fist in the palm of my hand."

I did like he said, only in slow motion. *Where's this going?* He wrapped his soft, fleshy fingers around my fist and shook. "Do you see?" he said. "You stuck it."

"What, you mean like Paladin kids are doing this?"

"No, kids in society. Kids like you do this, yes. I hope I did it right. It is a friendly gesture. Did I do it too soon? Should we be better acquainted before such customs?"

"I'll be honest, I never heard of it."

"You have not?" His head looked yellow again, splattered with specks of black. "My data says this is very popular."

"Where'd you get the data?"

"The data originated from a teenage website named Pops. It is rated the number one virtualmode website for teenagers in your age bracket."

"There's your problem. Pops is for little teeny girls and boys wanting to meet their favorite boy bands and movie stars. About as stupid as it gets."

"Is that true?" The colors changed. "I will have to rewrite my database."

"Good idea. And don't ever do that gay handshake again."

"Please do not curse, Master Socket. It is unbecoming of you."

"I didn't curse."

"I believe you did when you used the term 'gay' as a derogatory reference."

Now the colors on his faceplate were dark. I was being scolded by a robot. And he wasn't moving until I complied, I think. "Yeah, okay. No problem. Consider the word erased."

"Very good." The faceplate brightened. He stepped aside and gestured to the door. "Let us proceed to security assignment."

We went through the same door as Mom. It was an elevator.

"This is a leaper," Spindle said. "It will take us to any part of the Garrison in a matter of seconds. It can move as fast as two hundred miles per hour."

"Two hundred? We'll be pancakes."

"Not to worry. Anti-gravity floaters offset the velocity. You will not feel motion." Spindle stepped inside. "This is

39

the main mode of transportation within the Garrison. Centuries ago, when the Paladin Nation was in its infancy, these were just tunnels. Technology has advanced."

"Yeah. No shhhi...no kidding. I take it this thing wouldn't go anywhere without clearance."

"You would not be here if you did not have clearance." It seemed like he was refraining from laughing at something so stupid because, clearly, you're not getting here without a wormhole and a flying car. "Spindle, access code 0452B. Security assignment room, level 1. Prepare for new arrival."

There was a sharp pang in my stomach, and then it was gone. The door opened to a short, doorless hallway. So far I'd been in a cave and now a white hallway. For all the technology, Paladins weren't flashy.

Spindle started down the corridor and stopped halfway. "Here we are."

"Where?"

"Doors are composed of plasmic particulates creating the illusion of a solid surface." He pushed his hand through the white wall in front of us. "Much like the cliff you drove through."

I knocked on a solid wall. "It's not working."

"That is because you are touching the wall." His face lit with sunny yellows, shaped a little like a smile. *Dumbass.*

"Are you laughing at me?"

"Laughing? I do not experience emotions, Master Socket. However, it does appear odd you are trying to push through a wall when the doorway is right next to you."

"Yeah, well I don't see a doorway."

"Not yet." He walked through the wall, poked his head out several seconds later. "Are you coming?"

"I'm not used to walking through walls."

"Here." He extended his hand. "I am programmed to assist you."

An odd color lit his face. He lightly pulled me through —like a sheet of frigid air—into a large room. It was empty and sterile. How exciting. Let me guess, dinner is white rice with water.

"This is the security assignment room. I will assign you level one access. If you will have a seat, I will start the process very soon."

"You mean, on the floor?"

Spindle crossed the room in five steps. As he did, it reshaped. A chair emerged from the wall. End tables popped out of the floor. The white walls turned dark green with burnt orange trim. Pictures formed on the walls with views of oceans and deserts. A window appeared with the view of scenic mountains, a flock of birds passing by.

"Now that's what I'm talking about." I sat on the chair, felt it reform to fit my body, left me weightless. "This room… it's made from the same stuff as those servys?"

"Yes." He was busy with a control panel on the wall. "Our rooms can suit any purpose. I hope you are comfortable. We will begin in a minute."

A vase emerged from a table with flowers. I took a white daisy and sniffed. It smelled like a flower. The room was a regular room in any house across the world, and yet it wasn't. It was buried in a mountain made up of tiny cell-sized robots that made a flower smell like a flower and a window overlook a mountain. I could dig this.

"Can I ask you something?" I said.

"You may ask me a question at anytime, Master Socket."

"What's my mom do?"

"She is the Commander's assistant."

"Commander? You mean this is like a military?"

"It is not a military, but it has order. There is protocol. Any society must have rules and it must have leaders. Commander has been traditionally used."

"So my mom, she's a Paladin?"

The eyelight circled to the back of his head and focused on me while his hands continued to work. "No, Master Socket. Paladins have inherent abilities which she does not possess. She has developed some mild extrasensory powers but she is a civilian, and she is vital to the Paladin Nation. Has she not told you these things?"

"We don't talk a whole lot."

"But she is your mother." He stopped working. "Your caregiver."

"She's been a little busy. Since Dad died."

His face sparkled. "I knew your father."

"You did?"

"Yes." His eyelight drifted upward, thinking. "Your father was a remarkable man. He was head of mech design and maintenance. Your father was involved in my prototype design and personally worked on my bodyshell."

"He was a Paladin?"

"He expressed Paladin traits, much more than your mother, but never fully realized them. He worked in the Garrison and was not often involved in missions. The Paladin Nation has been watching to see if you would inherit his traits. I believe you caught them by surprise."

"What's that mean?"

"All the details will be revealed to you soon."

My dad died in for a secret agency and no one ever told me. That's super. No doubt she knew I was next line to follow in his footsteps. What else did Mom have in the family vault?

I buried my face in my hands and took a deep breath. *I want off the crazy train.*

"Was he a good father to you?" Spindle asked.

To me? He was asking like my father was a good father to him. Did he think we were brothers? I shook my head, my voice echoing through my hands. "I guess. I don't remember much."

"I remember your father quite well, from the very first day he ignited my awareness panel." His eyelight drifted up, again. He was lost in thought for several seconds while colors flashed on his face. "We spent every day together in the beginning, perhaps the entire first year of my existence. He worked on my programming to perfect my learning impulse. After that, I saw him once a week. That is unusual, you realize, for a creator to remain after programming is complete. Your father did that."

He had that drifting look again. "You miss him?" I said.

"Miss him? I am not sure what you mean."

It feels like there's something missing, that's what. It's longing. Sadness. It's all of the above. "It feels... empty."

"Empty?" He contemplated that, feeling his belly with his hand. His face brightened in a *got it* moment. "There is something missing. A... hole in my awareness. Not a hole, but an..." His eyelight focused on me. "*Emptiness.* Yes, I do sense that. I do miss him, Master Socket. Thank you for teaching me."

The colors on his face ran through the full spectrum, brighter and brighter. I didn't consider emptiness as something he needed to thank me for. For me, it ached. But for Spindle, it was obviously something joyous to experience. *Whatever.*

He turned back to the control panel. Then said, "If you hold still, a body print is being scanned and a security access level assigned."

Tiny shockwaves started at my feet and ended at the top of my head. The control panel folded back into the wall. The pictures, vase and flowers dissolved. I stood and the chair disappeared. The room was empty, once again.

"You have been assigned level one access." Spindle walked through a dim arching outline on the wall. I could see the doorway now. No more walking into walls for me. I followed him into the hall.

"You should be able to see doorways to rooms you have clearance to enter," Spindle said. "Do you see them?"

There was a similar outline that simulated a doorway at each end of the hall. I nodded. "Got it."

"Good," he said. "Agent Pike is waiting."

"Agent Pike? Who's that?"

"He will be conducting your preliminary evaluation."

"Whoa, wait a second. I thought we were going to Mom's office. I don't know anyone named Pike."

"All potential cadets are evaluated for potential traits upon arrival. It is the first assignment after security clearance."

"I'm a cadet? Wait, when did that happen? I didn't sign up for anything."

Spindle remained absolutely still, assessing the conversation. "Why do you think you are here, Master Socket?"

"I don't have a clue."

Long pause, again. "You were assigned to the Garrison because you exhibited exceptional abilities that need to be assessed."

"When the hell did I do that?"

His face darkened, but he let the *hell* word slide. "It will all be explained to you after the preliminary evaluation. However, it is imperative that we remain on schedule. You need to report to Agent Pike immediately."

I grabbed him as he turned. "Wait, I'm not going anywhere until you tell me what's going to happen at this... evaluation."

"Agent Pike is a minder; he has extraordinary psychic ability. He will assess your potential."

"So I *am* a Paladin?"

Pause. "That is up to Agent Pike to decide." He stepped quickly before I could grab again. I was trapped in a short hallway inside a mountain about to meet a man named Pike. *It's just a little stick, Socket.*

We walked into a leaper at the other end of the hall. "We will be traveling at 189 mph in a northwest direction exactly 33 degrees above ground level, covering 5,133 feet. Are you ready?"

Hell, no. A falling sensation twisted my gut.

"We have arrived."

It was another short hallway, a gray archway at the far end. Spindle walked with his shoulders square, his head held high. My knees were unreliable, but I forced myself to follow. I wanted to hold his arm, but I wasn't going to look like a pussy. Even if I felt like one.

"You will have to enter alone," Spindle said. "I will wait here."

I brushed my fingertips across the chilly gray archway. "So you're saying he's just going to ask questions, nothing else?"

"Yes," Spindle said. "And assess you."

Assess me. Goddamn, I don't like the way that sounds. "Where's Mom?"

"She is sorry." His fluid voice faltered, just a bit. "She is very aware of you."

Was that supposed to calm me down? Don't tell me the truth or I'll freak out. I was turning numb and couldn't stop nodding.

"Agent Pike." Spindle patted my shoulder. "He is waiting."

The weakness in my knees was now in my chest. If I waited any longer, I was going to fill my shorts. As I saw it, there was no choice. Nowhere to run. *The nurse never says the shot's going to hurt. She'll say it's just pressure, that's all you'll feel.* I put my foot through the archway, felt Spindle's hand slip off my shoulder, and plunged to the other side. *But we all know that shot's going to hurt like hell.*

PIKED

Pressure.

It was around me as soon as I entered, wrapped around my body, dimpled my skin like a golf ball. A frail man sat on a chair, his hands on his thighs. Stubble shaded his scalp. His narrow sunglasses partially wrapped around his head, the lenses convex and black.

"Have a seat." His voice was clipped, cold and dry.

A similar chair emerged from the floor in front of him. I pulled it away. We didn't need to sit that close. Tiny cracks appeared around his mouth. *More pressure.*

[Agent Pike has mental pressure at level one. The subject is feeling discomfort, but seems to be controlling his nerve response unconsciously.]

The thought was in my head. I looked around the room, white and empty, and there was no one here except me and this gecko-looking nutjob.

Agent Pike twitched. Nothing noticeable. His eyebrows lifted a few microns. How did I notice that? *Gecko.* There, it happened again. He heard me. *Is that right, Mr. Gecko?*

"I am Agent Pike," he said, no warmer than his greeting.

A servy emerged from the wall. Three arms grew from the middle of its body. I pulled my arm away. It stopped, turned its eyelight to Agent Pike.

"The servy simply needs to monitor your vital signs and take a few samples. It will be painless."

The eyelight returned to me. I could've fought the thing, but they were going to get samples one way or another. I had the feeling I was going to need all my strength by the time this "evaluation" ended. One of its arms wrapped around my elbow, turning it numb. The other two arms touched various parts of my back, neck, and chest.

"You performed an unauthorized timeslice today at 11:25 a.m.," Agent Pike said.

"Yeah, I didn't do anything."

"Timeslicing is a stoppage of relative time. Since this incident, you have heard random thoughts. Has this not happened to you?"

I don't like this guy.

"We know this to be true, but your cooperation will make this transaction easier."

He didn't need me to answer. He *wanted* me to answer. So I nodded. Fine. There's your *transaction,* weasel.

The servy pulled its rubbery arms off, merged back into the wall. Three spots of blood beaded on my arm. *Blood, skin, tissue, muscle. You forgot a chunk of brain.*

Agent Pike eyebrows shifted again. *More pressure.*

The dimpling sensation was deeper, more intense. I grabbed the bottom of the chair. A line of sweat popped up on my lip. That last wave went deep, like the dentist forgot to numb me before drilling.

"Only Paladins have the ability to cease relative time," he said. "It is not magic. We have the ability to alter our metabolism to move and think infinitely faster than the ordinary human, to *experience* time stopping. The ability can be performed only in short bursts before the body consumes all its energy. You were very hungry after timeslicing, were you not?"

He paused. *We know this to be true.*

"Your timeslicing ability was activated by an unknown presence that approached in the form of a shadow. This person was traced to the Garrison, but we do not know the identity." His nostrils flared, blowing hot air. "Tell me who the shadow is."

I barely remembered what happened; how would I know who the shadow is? This guy was a moron if he thought—

My eardrums popped. The air thickened.

"You are sixteen years old." Agent Pike's voice was now unusually loud, slightly echoing. "Paladin cadets do not timeslice until they are twenty. Your activation is an anomaly." His lips moved softly, no more than a whisper, but the words rang. "WHO ARE YOU, SOCKET GREENY?"

[Agent Pike, back down the mental pressure.]

His stare locked me in the chair. I couldn't move. It was a full blown seizure. The chair legs rattled.

[Agent Pike! You are ordered to back off! The subject is unstable; you must stop the pressure immediately!]

A black tunnel collapsed around me. My head split. No, not my head. *My mind.* Pike went looking for answers. Psychic fingers pushed inside like cold spikes. I let out a howl that died in the dense air. Memories hurtled out of the blackness, falling at random. Things I'd forgotten played like movies.

Two years old. Dad pulled me from the car and Mom came around. The room was large and dank. Musty. *The parking cave.* Dad carried me and his footsteps echoed. A man greeted him. Shook his hand.

"He's showing signs," Dad said.

The man ruffled my hair. His breath minty. I hid my face in Dad's shoulder. "We'll keep an eye on him," the man said.

Icy pain cut me. Pike dug deeper.

I was four, holding Dad's hand. The carnival lights illuminated the night that smelled like straw and sugar. I ate something fried on a stick. Dad tore off a piece, popped it in his mouth. "You want to go on that one, Socket?" he said.

A capsule ride shot straight up, disappeared above the lights.

"Trey," Mom said. "I don't think that's a good idea. He'll get scared."

I held his rough hand and we climbed inside the capsule. It was humid and smelled like puke. We strapped into the seat and I was thinking Mom was right. I grabbed Dad's arm when we blasted off, buried my face in his coat.

"It's all right, Socket," he said. "It'll be all right."

Mom waited for us when it was over. She was wringing her hands but she was smiling. *Smiling.*

Pike plunged deeper. Memories popped like bubbles, overlapping each other. Confusing one with the other. I was spinning. Faces passed. Days went by. The memory wheel stopped.

I was five. The colorless sky was cold.

Men were dressed in dark uniforms with white gloves, standing in line. They lowered a casket into the ground, draped a flag over it. Dirt thudded on the lid. A few people cried, but most were expressionless, like soldiers that knew the line of duty. Mom was dressed in black. Her face was sallow. Eyes were sunk in the dead zone.

A man rustled my hair. "Your father was a good man."

His breath was minty. My stomach was hard and cold, that block of ice I would carry the rest of my life had already formed.

Memories fell faster, each one stacking on top of the next. Pike flipped through them like playing cards, each one ripped from somewhere dark and quiet. The catalogue of my life reeled in front of me.

I was tearing.

He was coming in. I couldn't keep him out. I wasn't big enough to contain him.

The memory of the Rime appeared, fast forwarded to the shadow. The view was fading. Pike grappled with the memory, trying to bring it into focus. His mental fingers grew colder. Sharper.

WHO IS THE SHADOW?

It just hurt.

Too much.

"You are not authorized to enter this room!" Pike slithered out of my mind.

I was back in my skin, slumped in the chair. Empty and violated. Several people entered the room, emerging from the seemingly solid walls. Their hair was short. Their uniforms tight and black. Two of them wore black glasses. They stepped on each side of Pike like bookends. Pike jumped up, his chair falling back and dissolving. Spindle wrapped his arms around me and kept me from falling.

"You were ordered to back down twice!" Mom shouted. "YOU WILL NOT BREAK HIM!"

"I am in charge of this preliminary!" Pike retorted with equal venom. "You have no right to be in here!"

"He is my son!" Mom shot back. "And this has become a psychic lynching! You were not authorized to probe deeply!"

"There is a traitor in the Garrison. I will use whatever methods necessary."

"This preliminary is over. You will be removed from this assignment."

His face reddened. "I am primary minder. I decide methodology. I assess traits, my decisions are final. Understand, *civilian,* I will not go."

"You can have this conversation with the Commander, if you like, but either way, we are finished."

Pike turned, the glasses slipped, revealing white eyeballs. No iris. No pupil. He fixed his glasses and stared at Mom, but she didn't flinch. She stood in front of me, her hands clenched. Veins pulsed in Pike's neck. Tension hissed.

"Try it." Mom stepped closer to him, her nose almost touching his. "Go on, get inside me and try it."

The room charged with static. Her hair floated out.

"If you dare to penetrate my mind, you will not see the outside of a prison cell for eternity, I will see to that, personally, Agent Pike. If you do not contain yourself in the next few moments and leave this room, I will bring a team of minders in here to incapacitate you for the rest of your life. If you don't believe me, then try it." Her lips were very thin. "Back. Down."

The vein throbbed on Pike's neck. A bead of sweat rolled down his temple. He calmly adjusted his black glasses. He sucked air between his teeth, took his time turning and glided through the wall. The two black glasses-wearing men followed as did three black suits. Two men stayed in the room, hands behind their backs. At attention.

My mind was still cleaning up the memories Pike uncorked, trying to put them in their rightful places. They swirled like papers finding their way back to the ground.

"Get him to the infirmary," Mom said to Spindle and the men. "I want a medical minder to begin decompression wave therapy immediately. Have the medical mechs monitor his vitals and administer sedatives but do not put him to sleep. Once normal brain activity resumes, I want him asleep for twenty-four hours. All activity is to be sent to my office, keep me updated of every second, Spindle. And I mean every second."

A stretcher floated inside the room. Servys laid me on it, guided it down the short hall to the leaper. Mom and Spindle walked along side.

"I will be updating Commander Diggs with what just happened," she said. "Contact all my appointments for the rest of the day and reschedule for tomorrow."

"But you have an appointment with the Director of—"

"I don't care," she said. "I need some time with the Commander."

I took her hand. It was hot. Wet.

She pushed her hair back. The rigid muscles loosened along her jaws and around her eyes. She stopped the stretcher before it went inside the leaper, squeezed my hand and pushed the hair off my forehead.

"You made it," I croaked.

She nodded, feeling my forehead. She whispered, "Get some rest." She stood back. "I'll be with you soon."

We moved onto the leaper. She watched from the hallway. She would not rest. Not tonight. There was too much to do.

II

Time does not exist.
There is only the present moment.

The past and future are merely thoughts about the present
moment. If you think about it, you have already missed the
point. One must live life in the present moment to be real;
otherwise, your life is a collection of thoughts.

No different than data.

PRESERVED

Weeks passed. Then months. Instead of getting on a bus for school and falling asleep in front of the TV, I was somewhere else in the world where they administered tests and I went to sleep on a weightless bed looking out so called windows with views of canyons, oceans or whatever scenic view was on tap for the night. Sometimes I forgot it was just a picture, that few things I saw were actually real. Then again, I wasn't trying to think all that much. If I really thought about what was happening, I'd unravel. So I did what they told me, went where they wanted me and shut up for once.

I thought a lot about Pike. Not so much the part where he tried to rip my mind in half, I tried to forget that part, but the question he asked: *Who are you?* I think he meant to find out if I was a spy or something, but I kept hearing it a different way. *Who am I?* I thought I was some sixteen year old latchkey kid growing up in a broken home. I figured I'd end up drilling holes in sheet metal for a living and die in a retirement home. Not exactly the American dream, but there were worse fates.

But now who am I? Really, *who am I*? Does anyone *really* know who they are? Are we just a collection of behaviors we learned as babies that run us around like wind-up toys? Or does anyone know why we're here? Is there a purpose to any of this besides getting a piece of gold and a boat and a hot wife to put on it? There has to be more to life than just this.

I sat in my little room sometimes pondering all that, but I always ended up on that one question: *Who am I?* Somehow it didn't feel like it had an answer, but it was a question that had to be asked. Over and over. If I didn't ask it, I felt crazy. And I had to hang onto every shred of sanity I could because this place made little sense. And everything I thought I was didn't exist anymore. *So who am I now?*

My testers were never the same person. Sometimes a man, sometimes a woman. Never Pike. Thank the lord in heaven. They were never friendly, never rude. They took blood samples, tissue samples, made me run, walk, do push-ups, asked some of the goofiest questions I've ever heard. "Have you ever noticed cockroaches following you?"

"What?"

He or she would ask the question again, almost as if they just wondered if I liked vanilla or chocolate ice cream.

Sometimes the interviews were more formal. We would face each other in chairs, they'd ask questions, I'd answer. Sometimes they would ask if I saw certain colors, or heard a certain thought. Sometimes, I did. I felt psychic pressure, but nothing like what Pike did; that was like a grown man trying to squeeze his fat ass into a baby's onesy. The testers would ask me to *open my mind* and asked what came up.

The first couple times I sat there and daydreamed. The third time, I *saw* something. It was like my mind had become a three-dimensional staging area. A reddish object appeared.

"What did you see?" the tester asked.

"An apple."

The tester said nothing. Wrote nothing down. But I was right. He was thinking of an apple and I saw it.

The next day, I knew how to read thoughts. That's right, I could look into someone's mind and see what they were thinking. I could even shut the thoughts out, if I wanted. It wasn't doing me a damn bit of good around the Paladins that had full control of their thoughts. Opening my mind to them was like trying to find out what a wall was thinking. But I could read their thoughts if they let me.

"How do I stop time?" I asked.

The tester sat quietly, hands on his thighs. "You will have to look deep inside yourself," he said, calmly, softly, almost mechanically. "Inside there will be a metaphorical mechanism, a symbolic trigger, you can use to alter your metabolism. Some experience this as a spark found in the solar plexus."

I closed my eyes, focused on my gut. I remembered that sparkly feeling I had at the Rime, the first time I sliced time. I searched this part of my being but felt nothing but chaotic energy. I imagined I was a traveler, hunting a valuable gem, flying through inner space. Lights blurred past, curled out of my grasp like hyper fireflies. I went after them, one direction then the other, but they were nothing but tiny lights. No spark.

"You cannot chase it," the tester said. "You must allow it space; then, it will appear."

So I sat there. Minute after minute went by. Pretty soon I was thinking of lunch because the food in that place was outstanding. I could order just about—

"Bring your focus back."

I went back to my mid-section and let the fireflies do their dance. They stopped running away and began circling around me. Faster and faster they went, streaking inner space with curves brilliant and lasting. There was a twinge. My ears pricked with excitement. A bright light sparked. It was small and intense, like a quasar glowing somewhere inside. I brought all my awareness to this tiny flare.

"There." The tester barely spoke. "Wrap yourself arounddd..."

My hands involuntarily clenched. The spark grew brighter. Brighter, still. And then it happened. The spark ignited, engulfing me in a psychic blast. When I opened my eyes, the tester was still, his mouth partially open, caught in mid-sentence. I looked around the room for more proof, but I turned cold. And hungry.

"You are not strong enough to sustain a timeslice." The tester was standing over me with the hint of a grin. "But you found it. Nicely done."

No one would tell me what they were looking for when they tested. Told me nothing, in fact. Not who the Paladins were or what they were trying to protect the world from. Mom was the least helpful. I saw her more in those months than I had the previous year, but she had only one answer for every question: "I can't tell you anything right now, Socket."

I thought about Streeter and Chute a lot. We'd been friends forever, like family. Chute and I were, as Streeter put it, a girlfriend-boyfriend thing. I missed them both. Maybe I should've missed her more. I tried to call them, but the nojakk no longer worked. The Paladins shut it down. Standard procedure. Maybe they were afraid I'd call and say *You'll never guess where I'm at! I can stop freaking time!* I probably would've.

I wondered if they were worried. Not so much Streeter, but Chute. What was she going to think when she heard I was a freak? Who was I kidding? She was never going to find out. She might never see me again, even if Mom said I would see her soon. *Soon.* That was as specific as she got. That could mean *never.*

In between tests, Spindle and I played games. We played chess with holographic pieces and ping-pong on a table that materialized from the floor, complete with paddles and ball. He taught me a game called Reign. The animated pieces moved around seven levels of chess boards and chopped each other to pieces. Blood would squirt and the pieces would die moaning. Very cool.

I was restricted to the transforming rooms, leapers and corridors. No matter what shape or form they became or what illusory views I could see through the windows, it was stuffy. It beat school, yeah. And it beat sleeping in front of the TV on empty pizza boxes. But no matter how big the room, I was still inside a mountain. I hadn't seen the sun in a long time. Pictures of it, sure, but not the *real* thing.

"You have been cleared to enter the Preserve," Spindle announced in the third month, I think. For all I knew, we weren't even on a twenty-four hour schedule anymore. He waited for me outside a testing room where a man had asked if I could move a set of round objects with my mind (he gave me ten minutes but all I did was stare at them and wonder what he did for fun). Stupid.

I stepped quickly to keep up with Spindle, his gait so smooth and effortless. "Recreation is important," he said. "I think you will enjoy this very much."

We stepped inside a leaper.

I didn't know what a Preserve was, but it had to be better than staring at balls that wouldn't move. "No more tests?"

"You have no more tests today." The colors formed a rough smile on Spindle's face.

The leaper opened. I expected another white room, maybe a view (real or not) of the hills. At the very least, I'd hoped we might go out to the field Mom drove (or flew) across when she brought me to the Garrison. At least it was wide open. I just wanted to feel the wind on my face. We didn't go there; we went someplace so much better. We stepped outside where the sun was bright, the air humid and earthy. We were in the outside world, but one where I'd never been. One I never thought possible.

No illusion this time.

We emerged from the side of a cliff. From our vantage point, the tropical forest had been carved out of the mountain like a stone bowl. Trees, birds, palms... the whole deal.

"The Preserve is a man-made, enclosed environment supporting the growth of over ten thousand botanical species." Spindle spoke louder to clear the screeching call of a toucan or howler monkey or something else wild. "In addition, there are numerous exotic species of birds, mammals and aquatic creatures."

"Enclosed environment?" Blue sky was peaking between the clouds. "You mean that's not real?" My heart sank.

"Do you see those?" Spindle pointed to a barren limb on top of a large tree. "Those are magnashield generators disguised as part of the tree. There is one every five hundred square feet. They power an overhead force field that encloses the Preserve. Nothing can get in. Nothing can get out."

"How big is this place?"

"5.2 square miles. It is primarily used for research. Many medical breakthroughs that have been discovered here will soon be made available to the public. Right now, I would like to take you to the entertainment sector."

Spindle stepped onto a dirt path that went around an enormous banyan tree. The trail beyond the tree was 10 feet wide with a thick layer of leaves. Trees enclosed the humid path. Secondary paths split off now and again, darker and narrower. Things scurried along the undergrowth while small monkeys watched from above. One hung from a thick vine and screeched. Colorful birds teased him.

I'd been in places like that on a much smaller scale. We went on a field trip to a greenhouse conservatory with butterflies and lizards. Plants bloomed all sorts of colors, shapes and sizes, attracted bugs of equal strangeness. None of us said anything but *whoooaaaaa* for the first five minutes; then, we threw pebbles at turtles chilling on a log. But this was way beyond that.

Spindle stopped along the way, described plants, pointed at animals, and gave me the brief history of things he found interesting. I reminded him I was in high school, not college. But he was having too much fun, his faceplate all sunny and sparkly, so after awhile I let him do his thing.

We hiked for miles before stopping on a ledge and looking into the deepest part of the Preserve. There, surrounded by lush forest, was a large oval field of the greenest grass.

"Here it is." Spindle swung his arms out as if I'd won the grand prize. "It is a fantastic sport, a test of navigational skills, strength, agility, accuracy and teamwork. I am not one for guarantees, Master Socket, but I would wager it will be more popular than lacrosse, football, and soccer combined." His face lit with red, yellow and orange. "Tagghet."

"The game with jetters?"

"Yes. The technology has been in commercial production for a year. Perhaps you have seen it at your school."

"I've heard a thing or two."

"You have not played?" he asked. I just stared. "Then follow me."

The path switched back and forth. We dropped fifty feet in elevation before reaching the edge of the field. Spindle knelt on one knee and ran his hand over the grass.

"It is good fortune for a tagger to pause and touch the field before walking on it," he said.

"It is?"

"It is always good fortune to pause." He gestured to the spot in front of me.

"I'm no tagger, so I don't think so."

Spindle's feet sank in the lush, dense grass. The blades were narrow, the tips each holding a bead of moisture. Like living shag.

"This is nice," I said.

"I knew you would like it." His face sparkled. "The scent is quite grand, is it not?"

"You can smell?"

"I have olfactory sensors equivalent to a Labrador retriever."

I dropped to one knee and spread my hand over the turf, letting the wet tips tickle my palm. I wanted to lay in it and stare at the clouds like I used to with Chute and Streeter. We used to lay in my back yard, pointing at clouds and naming them, it was just us. Sometimes Streeter would have to go home and Chute stayed. She'd ask if I could read her mind, tell her what she was thinking. *You wish you had bigger boobs.* She left a red mark on my chest because I was probably right. Back then, there was no one else. No one judging, no one watching. We made up stories, laughed and played, and when we were ready to go home we did. No one was there to tell us, *Go here, now here. Make those stupid balls move with your thoughts.*

"If you are ready, we can explore the rest of the Preserve," Spindle said. "There are some magnificent features."

"Spindle, could I go alone?"

"You do not like my company?"

"That's not it, no… it's just… I just need to clear my head. I mean, my whole life changed in a single day and I'm still not sure I'm digging all this. I need to get lost for a while and sort things out. You know what I mean?"

"You want to… go without me?" His face turned dark blue. "I thought we would spend the afternoon together. There are many interesting things to visit. Creatures you have never seen. I was, perhaps, looking forward to showing them to you."

"Another time, huh? I'm sure I'll be here a few more weeks." *Or months. Years. Forever.*

He held out his hand and helped me up. "Of course. If you need help, I will come."

He said that like a Paladin angel. If things were just that easy in real life. *Is this real life?*

"I suggest you strike out on the path to our right. It will take you to an artificial sinkhole and a breathtaking water feature."

Spindle stood at the field's edge and watched me walk across the turf. I waved before entering the dense jungle. He waved back. Now if I could just see the clouds.

BATTY MAN

I was lost. Big time.

I could blame Mom for never putting me in Boy Scouts, but there was no badge for this. I made the mistake of getting off the trail. The trees all looked alike. My arms were scratched bloody. I sat on a rotten log to rest until fire ants stung the hell out of me. My legs were covered with welts. I went a bit further and heard the stream, went barefoot, stepping carefully on mossy stones. The cold water was a relief. I found a dry boulder. Checked for fire ants.

I was in a tropical forest. I couldn't see the sky, but it was still exactly what I had in mind. The lookits were somewhere and they were watching. At least, for once, it didn't feel like it. I was as close to alone as it was going to get. I was picking my nose, a full knuckle deep, and feeling pretty good about it. Until someone giggled.

"Who's there?" I called, oddly wondering if I could convince them I was just scratching my nose.

Something in a tree. Something bright red. A whole crew of things scrambled into the thick canopy, flashes of yellow, blue and purple. They crossed from tree to tree like squirrels. I splashed after them until the stream got deep and I went back on land. Spots of sunlight penetrated the trees ahead. I maneuvered around a tangle of vines and peeked through the leaves. It was a clearing, of sorts. A massive stone slab with patches of moss and snaky cracks. A huge tree was on the far side, its branches as big as tree trunks. The bark was twisted and sinewy, smooth and gray like a well-crafted relic. *Quite grand.*

The tree was without a single leaf, but alive with color. Thousands of bright colored creatures squabbled along the branches. Some crawled over each other, some wrestled, and others rested quietly. They didn't have feathers; they looked like bats, but their colors were like poison dart frogs.

Several of them hovered near a guy at the base of the tree. Spindle didn't warn me about other people in the Preserve. In fact, it was the first normal-looking person I'd seen who wasn't asking lame ass questions. He didn't look like he belonged here. His hair was long and his clothes ragged. He held up his hand and the creatures grabbed it. A fluorescent pink one hung by its long sharp tail.

I stayed in the trees and crossed the stream, didn't bother taking off my shoes. I hustled through the ferns, over rocks to a soft patch of leaves until I was a lot closer. The colored things were still there, but the guy was gone. They had little arms and legs and their tails swished like whips. They had snouts. *Caves and dragons. That was not a dream.*

I needed to get closer. I turned—he was behind me.

I fell through the branches onto the open slab and crawled backward. He stepped out of the trees. His skin was bronze from the sun, his hair bleached. And he wasn't a guy, he was more like a kid. Older than me, maybe, just out of high school. College?

"Who are you?" I said.

He flicked his sandy hair out of his eyes. His eyes... they were the eyes of a dead fish. He listened, held out his hand. I didn't move. He shook his hand, insisting I take it, so I reached up. He squeezed firmly, yanked me close. *Jesus, he hasn't showered in forever.*

He wouldn't let go. His pupils were much too large. He pulled me closer. Pressure gripped my entire body. I wanted to shake out of it but his eyes fixed me in place. They were deep holes. He let go. I stumbled, too dizzy to run.

"Are you all right?" someone said on my nojakk.

My nojakk was working. I tapped my cheek several times. "Hello?"

"Pivot would like to know if you are all right."

The blind guy had his face to the sun. Something moved over me like a thousand dishrags snapping on a clothesline. It was the things from the tree, slapping their leathery wings, stirring the dust at my feet.

"Can you speak?" I heard again.

A golden flying thing was on the guy's shoulder, its tail curled around his neck.

"You said that?" I asked.

"I did," the golden thing said without moving its mouth.

"How'd you do that... wait, you talk?"

"I do."

I stroked my cheek. "How'd you get my number?"

"We're good with technology." The golden thing shrugged. *"I did a simple scan, decoded your nojakk. You really should upgrade your passcodes."*

"Scanned it with what?"

"It's a mental scan. You wouldn't understand."

I'm reading thoughts and stopping time. Now there's talking... things. Sure, why not. "What are you?" I said. "Like a dragon or something?"

"*Phhsssh.*" Its lips flopped around, exposing rows of sharp teeth. "*We're grimmets, hailing from the edge of the Milky Way. My name is Sighter.*"

Grimmets. *Hmmmm.* Tiny dragons speaking on nojakks, apparently with their mind. We missed that species in biology class. And from the Milky Way? We missed that in astronomy. Of course, we never covered timeslicing in physics. I reached for Sighter, wanted to poke him, make sure he was real. He snapped my finger with his tail, like a wet towel.

"CHRIST!" A red line swelled across my knuckles. I put it to my lips. "Why'd you do that?"

"*We're not pets.*"

"Well, tell him that, you're sitting on his shoulder."

"*I like him.*" He wrapped his tail around the blind guy's neck again. "*But Pivot doesn't own me, boy.*"

"My name is Socket."

"*I know.*"

"Then why'd you call me boy?"

"*I just met you.*" He rolled his bulging eyes. "*Do I have to explain everything?*"

"Listen, three or four months ago I was living a normal life, now I'm reading thoughts and stopping time and you look like a golden dragon that did some sort of..." I waved my hands over my head, frantically, "*mental scan* to steal my passcodes and now you're talking to me, without moving your lips." We stared at each other, deadpan, until I said, "So, yeah, explain everything."

Pivot's eyes remained unfocused, but his lips moved. Sighter nodded.

"*Fair enough, boy,*" Sighter said. "*Follow us.*"

We went to the tree. It wasn't growing in the stone slab, after all, but against it. The slab dropped off and below, maybe fifteen feet, was a pond. The tree was rooted in that. Pivot sat against the tree and Sighter climbed to the top of his head. Hundreds of grimmets peeked out of hiding places along the branches, their eyes glowing.

"We came to help awaken the human race."

"This gets better every day," I muttered.

"You don't think Earth is the first planet in the universe to make a mess out of their evolution, now do you?"

"I didn't even know there was life on other planets."

Sighter shook his head. *"You have so much to learn, boy."*

"I just got here. Remember?"

The grimmets fluttered around Pivot like needy butterflies, fighting to be the next to swing on his fingers. Sighter stood on his shoulder monitoring the fracas, waving them off when they got too pushy.

"So who are you?" I asked the blind kid. "Your name is Pivot, right?"

No answer. Then all the grimmets looked up. Their eyes grew wider. Brighter. They scattered like bugs, found stones to sit on, branches to hang from. Sighter crossed his arms. They weren't looking at me. They looked over my shoulder.

Someone strode across the stone slab. He was about my age. Each one of his steps landed softly and purposefully. His hair was black, properly cut. His one-piece suit was loose fitting, green and beige. It may have been the colors of the jungle, but it was too clean to belong in the Preserve.

"Salutations," he said. "I see they have finally let you out of the box."

I was still taking in the camouflaged onesy and the strange way he walked. It was almost like he did it perfectly. Whatever that means. Guess he figured I was confused. He jerked his thumb over his shoulder, not taking his eyes off me. "The Garrison. They finally let you out. It can get quite stuffy in there, no?"

Not a single grimmet stirred. Pivot sat quietly, unnoticed. My gut sparked like a fire alarm just went off.

"I hope you don't mind, but I believe it is high time we met." He extended his hand. "I'm Broak."

I shook it. He squeezed my hand tightly, then quickly let go and rubbed it on his thigh.

"Your name is Broak?"

"Indeed, it is," he said, tipping his head. "I named myself. Didn't care for the name I was given, decided I needed something more regal and fitting. It is a combination of two of the greatest Paladin warriors ever to live: Braiden Alexander Faber and Stoak Glacial Ginshen. Braiden and Stoak." He pronounced each word crisply. "I am Broak."

"How about that," I stated.

Broak locked his gaze on me. I felt pressure surround me, push against my head. I set my feet, prepared for what might come next, but the probing was exploratory, not penetrating. It ran over my skin, under my chin, through my scalp.

"You have an unusual name, as well," he said. "Dear Socket."

"There's no dear. Just Socket."

"I see." Broak was humming to himself. Waiting.

"I don't think the name comes from anything," I said. "My parents liked tools."

People usually laughed at that. Not Broak. Maybe I should've made something up about a great warrior named Craftsman. He still wouldn't have laughed.

"You are creating quite a stir, you know." He narrowed his eyes. "The whole Paladin Nation is a buzz about the new find. I had to see you with my own eyes."

I filled an awkward silence with a laugh. He talked funny. "What's the big *stir*?"

"Well, for one, you are sixteen years old and timeslicing, my dear friend. That is quite abnormal. And so far your preliminary evaluations are soaring. Only one cadet has ever had higher scores than you." He smiled. Teeth perfect.

"And that would beeee... you." I gave him a chance to fill in the blank – he was obviously proud – but he let me do it.

"Do not feel disappointed. I am a product of genetic engineering. New and improved, one might say."

"You timeslice?"

"Oh, no. I will begin timeslicing when I'm twenty, that's the normal progression. You see, the body isn't prepared for such stress while it is still developing. At twenty, you are adept physically as well as mentally. You realize you are lucky to have survived your accidental timeslice." He smiled, again. A little too big. "Premature timeslicing can drain the life from you, starve you to the end. It is a good thing you are here for us to guide you."

"I'm thrilled," I said, thinking of my first day.

He opened his mouth wide and laughed. It sounded unnatural. Like he practiced laughing.

"Pike got a little aggressive in your preliminary, yes, I heard. You handled it quite well, though. Most cadets leave something like that unconscious. You, on the other hand, actually spoke. Quite impressive, indeed."

He looked me up and down, again; walked around. Grimmets scurried out of his way. He made a full circle, nearly stepping on Pivot. "Could you tell me something?" Broak held my hair, let it fall off his fingers. "Why is your hair so unkempt and lacking of color?"

This guy was way into my personal space. And he was holding my hair. That was... *unnatural*. My stomach tightened and sparked. Broak put his hands up like he felt a warning. *I surrender.* He rubbed both hands on his pants.

"Pigmentation disorder." I took a step back.

"I have never heard of such a thing. You are not albino, how is that possible?"

"I live in South Carolina but I'm standing in a jungle somewhere in the world where there's mountains. How's that possible?"

Suddenly, saying I lived in South Carolina didn't feel right. *Do I live here now?*

He stopped observing and narrowed his eyes. "You are intriguing, dear Socket. Take any other sixteen-year-old, drive him through a wormhole and introduce him to a brutal minder like Pike and, well, he'd be crying for mommy. You, on the other hand, behave as if this happens every day. You are quite extraordinary."

"Not like I had a choice."

"No. You didn't." His smile faded from his smooth face. No sign of whiskers.

"How old are you?" I asked.

"Same as you. Do you find that odd?"

"You seem pretty okay with all this yourself."

"That's because I was born here. I'm a Paladin breed. I was made to do this. You are a genetic mutation and that's why so many Paladins are all enthusiastic about you. They love mutations. They have this false hope that nature will provide the right combination of DNA to improve our race. But if you want to know the truth, you are just an abnormality, a random chance. If you think about it, it's like squirting paint on a canvas hoping it will become the Mona Lisa." He twitched. "Do you understand?"

Did I just get insulted?

Broak clasped his hands behind his back and looked into the pond below. He sniffed the air and sneered, then brushed a bit of dust from his chest. The grimmets rustled nervously, never taking their eyes off him.

"Whether you know it or not," he said without turning, "you are somewhere in between, dear Socket."

"In between what?"

"This world and the one you came from, where the regular people live." He looked over his shoulder. "I sincerely doubt you can go back. In case you haven't noticed, they don't know we exist."

Whether South Carolina was my home or not, I knew right then and there I didn't want to end up wearing a onsey in jungle colors. And the *dear* thing was really stepping on my nerves.

Broak walked along the rocky ledge. The grimmets stirred a cloud of dust getting out of his way. Broak glared at them crawling along the branches. He brushed his chest off again.

"You don't like this place," I said.

"I am not a fan of the Preserve," he said, wiping each arm, dutifully. "It is absolutely filthy. It is unorganized. Unpredictable. Pivot belongs here, not me. After all, the Paladins built it for him."

"They built what? That tree?"

"The entire Preserve."

5.2 square miles of tropical jungle, all for one person? "That's impossible."

He brushed both arms, both legs, licked the back of his hand and rubbed it off. Clean as a cat. Broak squatted next to Pivot, brushed the hair from his eyes. Pivot did not move.

"He is a mutant. Like you. Although you had the benefit of your father's association with the Paladin Nation, Pivot came from the general population. He was an accident. I suppose we found a Mona Lisa, after all." He looked at me. "What do you suppose the odds are of finding two?"

"Let's get something out in the open." My gut lit up. "Are you looking for a fight? Because it feels like you are, and I just met you."

The rehearsed smile creased his porcelain cheeks. "It's a great moment in history, dear Socket." He raised his hands in celebration. "I'm the perfect breeding. Pivot's the lucky mutt. And you... well, we're not sure what you are, just yet. Let's just say you show promise."

"Not that this matters, but I don't give two shits what you think. I don't care if I ever read another thought or stop another moment in time. You can drop me off back home, if you like. I was happy with my old life."

Then it hit me. *Happy with my old life?* Every day of my life felt like pushing a boulder up a hill waiting for something to happen. It was always that way, like I was missing what I was supposed to be doing. Now that I was with the Paladins, I didn't feel like a freak.

Broak pulled Pivot up and put his arms around us both. "Pivot's special. And I don't mean the he-can't-see kind of special, either. The Paladin Nation needs him. They need me. And, if what we've seen so far from your preliminary tests, you just might be special, too. Whether you like it or not, we have been chosen by a higher power to serve. All we can do is celebrate, dear Socket." He leaned close, his breath odorless. "Long live the Paladin Nation."

He shook us once, twice and let go.

"Now if you will please excuse me," he said, "I have to get out of this place. When you get some free time, join me on the tagghet field, won't you? I'll teach you the sport in no time. It will be worldwide within a couple years; you should know the rules, at the very least. And I must warn you, I'm quite good and I don't go easy on beginners." He smirked, the first sign of real emotion. "I'll give you quite a thrashing, but you will thank me for it later."

"When am I done testing?"

"They evaluated me in three days." He looked at Pivot. "They gave up on Pivot. You? Like I told you, you are somewhere in between." He winked. "Come see me when you can."

He walked down the slab. The grimmets hovered over me, watching. A red one landed on my shoulder. We looked at each other, both surprised at the sudden intimacy.

"By the way, you will have to clean yourself up," Broak called. "The white hair is odd but I like it, I really do. But you're going to have to clean it up. Better yet, cut it." He stopped at the edge of the trees. "And for God's sake, don't let those things sit on you, dear Socket. They live in the trees."

Broak walked into the forest.

Pivot was gone. So was Sighter. Hot, sticky fingers clung to my skin. The red grimmet walked to my other shoulder, wrapped his long tail around my neck. His gold eyes glittered. Blinked. The rest of the grimmets sat on the branches. Watching. Blinking. They started climbing into the holes, one after another, disappearing into the tree.

The red grimmet leaped off, flew after them. He marched down the branch, one of the last to go inside. One thought rang inside my head. It was a single word coming from the little red one.

[Rudder.]

The red grimmet's name was Rudder.

ORPHANS

Three days, my ass.

I had the feeling dear Broak was lying about his testing because mine was endless. Weeks went by and every morning I woke up hoping it would be over, only to be trotted to another tester and another boring day. I eventually turned my room into an exact replica of my bedroom back in South Carolina. My messy desk was in the corner and, next to that, an open door that led to the bathroom. If I didn't know any better, I would've gone to the kitchen to grab something to drink, but there wasn't a kitchen through that door. Just another short hallway with a leaper at the end.

"Himalayas."

The white space swirled inside a huge frame until wispy clouds hung on the icy capped mountain in the distance. It reminded me of the Rime. That's where it all

75

started. What if I didn't go there that day? Would the shadow have found me? Would I be laying around the house watching TV on a three-day suspension?

"Good morning." Mom walked in and looked around, ignoring my obvious plea to go home. *This is your home, Socket.* She put on a smile, a courageous attempt to mask the exhaustion, but her facial muscles just couldn't keep up. Did she even sleep anymore?

"I've got good news," she said. "I received clearance for you to meet Streeter and Chute on the Internet. You can virtualmode to a secure location and they'll meet you."

"You did?" I jolted out of bed.

"I did." She smiled back. "I know it's not the same as seeing them in the skin, but it's the best I could do. I'm not sure when it can be arranged, but soon."

There was hope after all.

"I want you dressed," she said. "Some testers arrived late last night to see you this morning and they need to leave by lunch."

Breakfast was anything I could think of. *Anything.* Eggs, slightly runny, a bowl of grits with two pats of butter and two and a half strips of bacon. I added a side of poached salmon just to screw with them. Two minutes later, a servy carried a piping hot tray that stunk up the room. I sent it back. *Okay, you win.*

I went to the test, this one with a man and a woman. I inserted my hands into special gloves and put on dark glasses. They gave me different scenarios and asked me to respond. "You find yourself in a room with three strangers. One of them is a murderer. The lights go out. Respond."

What am I supposed to say to that? If I leave the room, I'm a coward. If I kill them all, I'm the murderer.

"Am I the killer?" Tiny lights flashed, I saw some data roll through the dark glasses and heard some *mmmmm-*

76

mmm. That meant my answer was very interesting. Not necessarily right, but interesting.

I was starved for lunch. I sat in an ordinary white room at a long table, watching the news reports on a three-dimensional TV. I ordered peanut butter and jelly with a thick layer of spicy potato chips and sliced pickles. Spindle sat at the other end with his hands splayed out on the table. I continued eating. He continued watching.

"Tell me about Pivot," I said.

"I can only give the general background. You are not cleared to access his entire database."

Mmmmmmm... interesting.

"Master Pivot was found in a children's home. His parents were never seen."

"Has he always been blind?"

"Yes. According to the director of the home, he just showed up one day. The other kids named him Pivot because of the way he turned around without lifting one of his feet. Much of his time, according to the director, he spent sitting in a chair, as if observing. The other kids did not care to play with him. Some of the older kids assaulted him. After that, the director called the authorities."

"He called the Paladins?"

"No. The Paladin Nation monitors the world for suspicious activities. Once they secretly learned of Pivot, they took him without notice."

"Was he hurt?"

"There were screams from other children. When the director arrived in the bunk room, five teenagers were unconscious at Master Pivot's feet. The other children told the director that the boys were teasing him. They wanted him to take off his clothes. When they attacked, they began to spasm like they had touched an electrical wire. They convulsed for a minute before they went unconscious."

I was holding a half-eaten pickle. "He killed them?"

"No," Spindle said. "They recovered fully."

If they got a dose of what Pike had given me on day one, then hell yeah they were screaming. "What happened after that?"

"Master Pivot went through much of the same tests you are now experiencing."

"And he lives in the Preserve?"

"He does. At one time, he had living quarters much like yours, but he experienced extreme agitation. Since coming to the Preserve, he has stabilized."

"You know, Broak told me they built the Preserve just for Pivot." I wagged the pickle at him. "That's crazy talk, right?"

"Master Pivot is a very powerful cadet and, I might add, one of the most unique. He expresses minder potential and yet is not a pure minder. He is quite possibly the most powerful cadet alive, but it is not known how well he controls his abilities. The Paladin Nation is very patient with his development. They want him to be comfortable."

"What's so important about him?"

His faceplate became a mess of gray specks. "That information is classified."

I licked the peanut butter off my thumb and took another bite, remembering that, even though Pivot had dead fisheyes, there was a magnificent depth to them. It only took one look to know he was something special. And not the he-can't-see kind.

"What about Broak?" I asked. "What's he all about?"

Spindle's head dimmed, a deep scarlet line jagged on the lower half. "Master Broak's story is much different. He is the result of careful breeding, artificially conceived. He has been very promising, expressing his skills at an age earlier than anticipated. He is also very important."

"Believe me, he thinks he's important, too," I said. "He doesn't have parents?"

"He was raised by trainers."

Trainers, huh? There's a new concept. What could be worse than training the day you come out of the womb... or slide out of a test tube or hatch from an egg? He was built.

"So what he said is true?" I said. "He's the Paladin's darling."

"If test results are any indication, he will be a very potent Paladin. The Paladin Nation is currently cloning his gene sequence for future generations. Earth will be very secure under his leadership."

Spindle's faceplate turned pale, for just a second. *Under his leadership.* That was the company line. I don't think Spindle was on board with that.

"So what exactly are the Paladins protecting us from? Monsters? Aliens? Killer tomatoes?"

"I am afraid that information is classified."

"I'll bet its terrorists. Right?"

"I cannot confirm nor deny that statement."

"What's the big secret? Terrorists are blowing stuff up every day. Why do we need a secret police agency? I mean, they aren't keeping secrets. They just attacked some building the other day and told the whole world about it."

Spindle remained still for several seconds, perhaps contemplating what was classified. His faceplate brightened when he had the answer. "It is best that humanity does not know what danger it is in. They would be very unhappy. There would be mass chaos. Financial stability would collapse worldwide. No, Master Socket, it is better that we serve humanity without their knowledge. Keeping them safe is most important."

We keep the world safe, Socket, that's all you need to know. Mom always said that. *Secrecy leads to corruption.* That's what my Global Politics teacher always said. Of course, Paladins weren't ordinary people. That's what Spindle would say.

A servy fetched my empty cup. I was full.

PERFECT FIT

The tests continued. I had yet to see Streeter and Chute. Mom said she was working on it. But every day, no Chute or Streeter. Just tests. She promised it would work out, and I believed her. There was only so much she could do. They let me into the Preserve. Occasionally I'd hear shouts and whistles coming from the tagghet field, but I stayed away from that end. Broak could do whatever, as long as it didn't include me. I was more interested in finding Pivot but he was nowhere to be found. Spindle said that was pretty normal, said he often went missing. He wouldn't explain what *missing* meant. That, he said with a smattering of gray, was classified. Sometimes I thought I'd catch a glimpse of Pivot through the trees, but then it'd turn out to be nothing.

There was no more getting lost. The main trails were the easiest and the lesser-known ones were good for avoiding the scientists who lurked around doing research. Sometimes I made my own trail and fought dogtooth vines and razor-sharp elephant grass. I'd lose some skin and blood, but it beat being in the box. Although, once my arm went numb after getting scratched by some toxic-laced branch and I ended up in the infirmary getting lectured by Spindle to be more careful.

"You are not invincible," he said. "You must understand your environment."

One afternoon, after a morning of exhausting tests, Spindle went with me to the Preserve. He insisted on going first. With him in the lead, I made it to the stream without a scratch then raced ahead to the grimmet tree.

I slipped on mossy stones, crashed through the trees and skidded onto the slab. The grimmet tree was empty, but this time there was one waiting. A red grimmet sat on the lowest branch, his feet going *tom-tom-tom* on the wood. He was the only grimmet there, staring right at me. I started for him.

"Grimmets are not receptive to strangers," Spindle said. "You should let him come to you."

Rudder had given me his name. That meant something. I stopped several feet away, offered my hand. Rudder dropped off, flapped over and snagged my fingers with his tail. Hung like a possum.

"Where've you been?" I said.

He was breathing rapidly and loudly; purring shook my hand. I poked his round belly, tight and scaly, and the purring went right into my arm.

"You have a friend," Spindle said.

Rudder jumped onto my face and pinched my cheeks; his forehead pushed against mine, and he tickled my chin with his tail. Then he flew to the tree and pointed down. I went to the ledge. There they were, swimming and floating, some on the sandy shore. Pivot was at the far end with water up to his waist, washing dirt off his arms and face. His clothes were spread out on a rock. He looked skyward. Smiled. Why did it feel like I'd know him all my life?

"If you don't mind," Sighter said, fluttering in my face, *"Pivot would like to dress without you watching. He might live in the trees, but he still has a sense of modesty."*

A few minutes later, Pivot climbed up the tree wearing nothing but shorts. He moved effortlessly, muscles rippling down his back, along his arms and calves. Wet strands of hair hung over his face. He moved his head side to side, listening. Energy radiated from his skin that seemed to bend the light in a holy, aura sort of way. He continued to turn his head. Mild psychic pressure wrapped around me.

[Follow me.] His thoughts were big and loud in my mind and sounded much older than it should have. He pushed his hair back, exposing his milky pupils. Energy, sweet and filling, bubbled in my chest. *[I will show you things.]*

In one fluid motion, Pivot leaped off the rock, splashing into the deep part of the pond.

"Call when it's time to eat!" I shouted.

"But, Master Socket..." Spindle's voice trailed away.

I jumped without looking. My stomach lurched. I went several feet under and never touched bottom. I broke the surface trying to breathe, pulling in all the air I could to scream, "COLD!"

Pivot was in the trees with the grimmets swirling behind him. Insects fled for their lives. I swam to shore with Rudder hanging onto my hair. I ignored the branches and vines and followed. Pivot bounded over obstacles, swinging around tree trunks or running up them one foot over the other. Nothing slowed him. Few things cut him. I couldn't do what he was doing. If it weren't for the grimmets, I would've lost him. At one point, he was high in the canopies running along the limbs, crashing through the leaves like a parachutist falling to his death only to grab vines at the last moments.

When I couldn't even hear the grimmets, I stopped at a small pool to catch my breath. Was that the game? Catch me if you can? Well, I lost. And I doubted the lookits could even find me. Maybe that was how he went missing.

A tight, piercing whistle cut the jungle. A family of yellow, long-beaked birds stared back. I heard it, again. Directly ahead, the trees were full of color. Pivot crouched behind a tree, put his finger to his lips. I stepped carefully and quietly next to him. The grimmets were just as stealthy, silently crawling along the limbs. Their bright colors became muted and natural, blending into their surroundings.

Broak was on the other side of the trees, coasting over the tagghet field on a jetter at mid-field with something like a red stick on his shoulders that was curved at the end and held a yellow discus. *The tag.* Five bulbous servys drifted at the far end around a large shimmering blue dome. A brilliant green cube was suspended a few feet off the ground inside.

Broak sped up, banked toward the dome. The servys gathered in front. Broak juked left, spun right and sprinted wide. The servys reacted and changed their defensive arrangement. The stick flexed in the momentum of Broak's swing and the tag flung off the end, splitting a tiny gap between the servys, through the dome and into the green cube.

Goal. I guess.

Broak set up another play. The servys changed formation. Broak scored again, this time from thirty yards out. This happened over and over. Different formation, different attack. Same result. Each move was more difficult than the one before. Each shot more precise.

Why are we watching tagghet?

The servys formed a defensive wedge. Broak hunkered down like a bowling ball looking for the pocket. He spun left, then right, and just before he made contact, bounced wide left. The servys were set for a collision and unable to respond quickly enough to stop him. Broak was all alone, except for the one servy that intercepted his shot. Broak followed it with the stick over his head and chopped with both hands.

"I ORDERED YOU TO FOLLOW DEFENSIVE FORMATION 2B WEDGE!"

The servy retreated. Broak pummeled it again. And again. The club sank deeper with each blow, blobs spurting with each hack. It tried to evade every swing, but lost navigational direction and went in circles. Broak speared it through the center and twisted. The servy split open, spilling goo all over. Broak stomped the remains.

The remaining servys gathered in front of the dome, their eyelights bright red. Broak dropped the club and waved them off. They quickly dispersed into the trees.

A small hovercraft emerged from a path. A man in uniform handed Broak a towel. Broak held out his hands and the man in uniform sprayed them with a small bottle. Broak wiped his hands on the towel. The man gave him a second towel and Broak wiped his face. They spoke. The man stood rigid while Broak replied forcefully, banging his fist on his own leg. The man listened; said something back. Broak looked around, scanning the trees. He wiped his face, looked again. *He knows we're watching.* He nodded to the man. They got onto the hovercraft and left.

We waited a long time and no one moved. Pivot finally walked onto the field. The grimmets followed in a flurry. The gray material was melting like snow in August. Pivot scooped up the remains. He took my hand, dropped it in my palm. It was sticky. Cold.

Dead.

It was only a machine. There was no life to mourn. But Pivot sat there on his knees, head bowed. Maybe it wasn't the death he lamented. Maybe it was the killer. He didn't bring me to see tagghet, after all. *Understand your environment.*

He took the gray substance from me, placed it on the ground. By the time we stood, it was gone. Pivot looked at me, his face warm. I heard no thoughts. He spoke no words. He just looked at me with cloudy eyes. He was warning me, but more than that, teaching me. Respect life, was that it? Respect it in all forms. Those servys were afraid while they watched Broak gut one of their own. They raced off the field when they were released.

When Pivot seemed satisfied, he walked away.

ORPHANS, TAKE II

"I can't ride that," I said.

Three jetters lay on the ground. One hummed to life when Pivot stepped on it, hovering several inches off the ground. He drifted across the field.

"*Why not?*" Sighter asked.

"Because I don't know how."

"*Lame excuse.*"

"Why can't we just go on foot?" I said. "It seems stupid to ride these things. Besides, we'll have to stay on the paths, and what's the use—"

"*Just step on it.*" Sighter flew over me. "*And stop whining.*"

Pivot was already on the other side of the field. I stepped on the jetter. It bobbed under my weight, shifting back and forth to keep me upright. My feet magnetically locked onto the surface.

"All right, I'm on it," I said. "Now what?"

"You know how to virtualmode, correct? It's simple thought projection. Focus on a command and the jetter will respond."

I closed my eyes, visualized going forward.

"And don't close your eyes. You want to see."

He wanted to add *dumbass* to the end of that sentence. I tried it again and this time I floated up. The jetter teetered side-to-side. I held my hands out like a beginner, but already I felt more connected to it. I opened my mind, like reading thoughts, and mentally merged with the jetter. I kept my arms out, just in case, and crept over the field. By the time I reached the trees, I sped up and came skidding to a stop.

"Oh, man. This is easy."

"Your head is growing by the second," Sighter said.

I was going fast enough to die. The jetter was magnetically rooted to my feet. Pivot was ahead of me. I followed in his leafy wake. We stayed on the main paths then took the narrow ones. Pivot carved the turns like breaking waves. The grimmets filtered through the trees. There was one close encounter with a low-reaching branch, but other than that it was balls out blazing.

When we reached the far edge of the Preserve, we dismounted and climbed a narrow path up the rocky face, above the canopies. The ledge angled up and twice switched back. We were several stories up and kept going. I didn't think much about falling. Somehow, I felt safe and in control near Pivot, like he could do something if I did.

The path ended at an alcove several feet deep and sheltered from above. From our vantage point, we were well above the Preserve. White birds glided over the treetops. A blanket of fog lay in some of the low areas that looked like clouds. Miles away was the entrance to the Garrison.

The grimmets perched on nooks and crannies jutting from the rock. We sat on the ledge, dangling our feet. Pebbles chipped off, took flight to the bottom, glancing off the cliff along the way. The sun was behind us, changing the color of the sky from blue to purple and red. Pivot's face was turned up, his cheeks rosy orange. I could stay here forever and watch the shadows grow, feel the sun go down and wait for it to come back up. I don't know how long we were up there. We didn't speak. We just shared the moment in seamless silence until the sky was no longer glowing.

There was gentle pressure on my head, then I saw an image in my mind. The face of a woman. Her hair was bound at the back of her head, strands of gray poking out. Wrinkles cut her face. Her smile was much like his, quiet and undemanding.

"Your mother?" I asked.

He looked directly at me. The pupils engulfed the faded blue irises. It was like looking into his soul, a pathway through the solar system, deep and black and limitless. He reached out and closed my eyes. A dream appeared as clearly as if I were there. The woman was with a man. They were sitting on a beach around a smoldering fire. The water lapped near their feet and the fire hissed. A boy with blond hair, barely old enough to be out of diapers, slapped a stick twice his size in the water, wading out deeper and deeper.

The boy ran but the dad scooped him up, slung him over his shoulder like a duffel bag. The woman wrapped him in a blanket. The family watched the sun paint the sky.

What happened to them?

The scene dissolved. The mom and dad's face turned gray and lifeless. They died, but how and why I couldn't tell. Did it matter? I mean, they were dead and he was alone. That's how I felt. My father died, didn't matter how, just that he was gone. And Mom? Part of her died, too. At least I had a mother. A broken one was better than none at all.

Another vision began.

I saw my mom standing in my bedroom. I was five years old and fast asleep. Mom knelt next to me and dropped her head. She was sobbing. I never saw her cry, not once. Not at the funeral and never after. The dead zone took care of that. But in the vision she cried so hard my bed shook. She took my little hand and held it to her cheek.

I opened my eyes. "How do you know all that?"

He looked up, humming a song in his throat. It sounded familiar. Felt soothing, like a lullaby. He didn't answer my question. Somehow, it seemed he knew me better than I knew myself. Maybe he didn't know what happened, he simply showed me a memory that was buried in my mind. He uncovered it for me to see.

How many other things were buried inside me?

INSIDE THE MACHINE(S)

I woke the next morning in a bed. No trees. No sky. Just a white ceiling. The visions from the Preserve were still fresh. I revisited the memories, over and over. It only made me long for escape, but I couldn't stop recalling. I could still envision the vast treetops and settling fog and the sun casting strange colors in the sky. Mother crying.

"Room?" I called.

"Yes?" a woman's voice answered.

"Are there any records of my father?"

"Yes. Most are classified."

"Show me what you got."

A faint magnetic field passed through the room. A hologram appeared next to me, a man six feet tall. His goatee was sprinkled with gray, his white hairline receding. I stood on my toes and looked into my father's eyes. I reached for his hand to see if it was callus but I passed through the illusion. The image shrank in scale to reveal him standing in a workshop.

"Trey Greeny was an exceptional student in circuit mapping and gel intelligence," the room said. "He was promoted to advanced standing and level four security clearance by the age of twenty-two. He was awarded the Medal of Commendation for his bravery in the sector five space attacks."

Space attack?

Dad shut a panel and ran a welding pen over the seam. A servy retrieved the tools on the floor. There was no sound from the image. He looked like he laughed, waved someone over.

"Trey Greeny completed 204 deep-space missions while employed at the Garrison. He was married to Kay Greeny and had a son named Socket."

Another man entered the scene. He could've been a Paladin, but the hair was down to his shoulders. I walked around to get a better view.

Pivot.

Dad showed him something on the workbench. The room continued with details about his everyday life, stuff my mom told me over the years. Stuff everyone knew. But all the good stuff was classified. Space missions. Inventions.

Spindle entered the room.

"Pivot knew him," I said. "Why didn't you tell me?"

"You did not ask."

"Didn't you think I'd want to know?"

"I do not see thoughts, Master Socket."

"Well, you can use logic, can't you?" I said. "It doesn't take a genius to calculate that I'd want to know about my father!"

I get tested for this and that and no one explained anything. Bullshit.

91

"There is not much to know." Spindle's face was blue. "Pivot has always been withdrawn, but he responded to your father. The Paladin Nation encouraged their relationship in hopes Pivot would fully develop."

"Develop? What's that mean?"

"Pivot emits an extraordinary level of psychic energy. He is a minder of another breed. His energy has a profound impact on other Paladins. His presence increases other Paladins' powers."

"So they're using him. They're leeching off him, is that it? They're taking from him, does he know that?

Spindle's face turned many colors. "Pivot provides the Paladin Nation with precognition."

"He can see the future?"

"It is not so much the future, but a deduction of events to come."

"Deduction of events..." I shook my head. "That's the *future*, Spindle. He's helping them see the future."

"The odds of future events," Spindle said, proudly.

No wonder they built him a jungle. He gave them the ability to see what would happen. There was no limit to that. They were rich: building a jungle for the future was a wise investment no matter how many trillions of dollars it took.

"So that's why they keep him," I said. "They're using him to watch the future."

"They are not using him like a tool, if that is what you mean. Pivot is a remarkable and highly valued cadet..."

He blabbered the company line, again. Instead of *remarkable and highly valued* he should've just said Pivot was a great commodity. Getting a real answer from Spindle was impossible. He was programmed, after all. He said what the programmers wanted him to say. He couldn't say what they forbid him to say. He had to follow the script. Every meaningful question just led to another standard answer, never a real one in sight.

He had the answers I wanted, but he wasn't programmed to give them to me. I didn't have security clearance. If I could bypass the programming, I could get to them. Or I could just take them. The Paladins taught me how to read thoughts. *What about machine thoughts?*

I opened my mind to the present moment. Let things present themselves. My consciousness expanded in a way it never had in the presence of a tester. I was growing. My personal energy filled the room. I touched everything. Knew it intimately. Inside. Out. My mind touched Spindle, wrapped around him. He experienced pressure. Spindle remained still, his face a curious color. There would be no time to get all the answers; he would surely shut down before I could. I had to make time.

The timeslicing spark twinkled. I didn't know what I was doing, but if I was going to do this, it had to be now.

I entered the spark.

My fists clenched. My body ignited from the inside. Spindle was still. Time, for me, had stopped.

I closed my eyes and expanded more. I left my skin like virtualmode discs pulled me out, but I didn't go to the in-between. I was my own captain. I floated from my skin like a ghost and entered Spindle's psyche. His thoughts were different from people thoughts. They were lined up, all connected in a purposeful directive, like an assembly line, destined for execution. But there was so much of it, I couldn't comprehend it. It wasn't like walking into a room and looking around; the mind was another dimension. I *felt* the thoughts, *tasted* them. They merged with my awareness. One or two thoughts were easy to absorb and comprehend, but Spindle was filled with a massive amount of data. There was no telling which thoughts allowed him to walk and which ones were top secret.

So I absorbed them all.

An avalanche of data filled me. My mind swelled. I heard things popping inside me. I teetered off balance, fell over, holding myself up against the wall. It was a paralyzing brain freeze that immediately started to thaw as the new information, the new experience of another's mind, trickled into my mind and found some sort of order. I stayed open for anything about my dad, but I stumbled onto something so much bigger. The information floated before my mental eye like a juicy nugget of gossip.

I saw what the Paladins were protecting the human race from.

The Paladin Nation has had many enemies throughout history, but they were usually human. And if the enemy wasn't human, it was at the very least living. For the first time, Paladins were faced with an enemy that imitated life.

I returned to my skin, released my grip on time. "Du..." My mind was coming back from the overload, reconnecting with basic functions, like standing and talking. I grabbed a chair to keep from falling. It took a second for my tongue to work. "Duplications are in the *skin*?"

"Master Socket," Spindle said, softly. "You breached my database... that is against—"

"The Paladin Nation is protecting the world against... FAKE HUMANS?"

"I cannot—"

"How the hell does a duplicated identity get out of virtualmode and WHERE THE HELL DOES IT GET A FREAKING BODY!"

"There is much humans do not know about their own world."

Three servys emerged from the wall and surrounded Spindle. His head and shoulders slumped.

"Get out of here!" I waved at them like flies. "We don't need assistance, leave!"

Spindle turned to exit, a servy on each side.

"Wait! Where're you going?"

He stopped. The servys came to an abrupt halt. "I will need to be reprogrammed."

94

"Reprogrammed?"

"My database has been breached. It will need to be reinforced to prevent that from happening again." His eyelight looked to the floor, his faceplate dark blue. "You are more powerful than estimated, Master Socket."

I grabbed his arm. "You're coming back, right?"

"I will come back." He patted my hand, like Mom did when something bad had happened. Or was about to.

I looked around the room, hoping I was making eye contact with whoever was watching. "I swear I won't do that again." An arm grew from one of the servys and took Spindle's hand. I refused to let go. "I'm not letting go unless you promise to bring him back."

We played tug of war. Spindle jerked back and forth. Two more servys entered. I shifted my weight, prepared to kick them across the room. Spindle's eyelight was bright. He gently took my hand and removed it from his arm.

"I will return, Master Socket."

His eyelight rotated away. The servys escorted him from the room. I would've done anything to take back what I did. I wanted to know why I'm here. I wanted to know what they are doing with me. I wanted to know about my father and Pivot. Instead, I discovered a titanic war.

I was ushered to a secure room, maybe it was an infirmary, I don't know. I don't remember. Once the adrenaline wore off, I was spinning in thoughts, not knowing which ones were mine and which were Spindle's. All I know is that I was lying down, staring at the ceiling like a mental patient. Eventually, Spindle's knowledge settled like grains of sand in a jar of water.

And then I understood. I understood it all.

When duplication first started however many years ago, the duped identities were set loose in virtualmode environments. People didn't think much of it; it was kind of cool knowing there was an exact duplicate of you that lived a separate life, even though it was digital. They were virtual clones and they were perfectly linked to whoever cloned them. The creator knew exactly where they were and what they were up to.

But anomalies in code developed, the human equivalent of genetic recombination, which allowed the dupes to break the link and roam free. They started living their own lives and their identities began to drift away from that of their creator. Dupes knew they were reproductions. They knew they weren't real and neither was their world. They wanted more than a virtual environment, a reflection of the physical world. They wanted to see what real life was. They didn't want to be told how the ocean breeze smelled or what love felt like, they wanted to know and not be told what an apple tastes like. They wanted the direct experience. They wanted to *exist*.

Dupes sought out their creators and attempted to download into their skin bodies, not to merge with them but to hijack their creator's skin. That's when the deaths spiked. People were dying at the hands of their own creations, their own selves. Their dupes were killing them.

Paladins discovered the new threat and secretly made the general population aware of it, but before duplication was eliminated and banned, the existing ones went into hiding. Virtualmode was a seemingly endless universe, but the Paladins were tracking them down. Dupes were being snuffed out. If they wanted to exist, they would have to escape virtualmode.

They found their way into factory networks that specialized in experimental textiles, specifically nanotechnology-based textiles, the very stuff that made up the moldable servys and Garrison rooms. Dupes, speaking the same language as computers, were able to download into the moldable material and secretly form human bodies without the factory operators being aware of it. They assumed bodies that grew hair, sloughed skin cells, sweat, shit and spit; they were indistinguishable from real humans, the organic soul-filled bodies, that were operating the factories and they walked out into the real world with a real sense of smell, taste, touch and sight. They escaped into the physical world. They were alive, and they were among us.

The Paladins caught on but too late. So many had escaped and blended into the population. The manhunt continued. The dupes remained fugitives and dispersed, disappearing into the human population like a cup of water dumped into the ocean. The only way for them to survive was to eliminate their enemy. *Humans.* With computer-like intelligence, they knew they could not win an all-out war. Brutality would be the weakest approach. Real power was of the mind. They surmised the key to defeating the human plague, as they saw it, was from the inside.

Win their heart, then destroy their mind.

Dupes used subversive methods to multiply their numbers. They created their own duplicates, and duplicates of those duplicates. They found ways into government, universities and major companies. Eventually, they would become a political party. Paladins had done the analysis, they consulted the future through Pivot, and discovered that dupes would take control of the world's most powerful nations within a decade and embark on the genocide of the human race. There would be no gas chambers, no firing lines or gallows. The dupe race would become the doctors that treated us and the cops that protected us. They would be our teachers and lawyers, our neighbors and friends. We would die of untreatable diseases and unstoppable terrorism. It would appear that some people were immune to the new age plagues, but in actuality, those that were immune weren't human at all. Eventually, there would be no humans left.

The human population wouldn't even see it coming. Dupes would be a master predator. Humans would not even know they had been hunted. As the Paladin Nation saw it, the human race would be extinct in twenty-seven years.

Without the Paladins, the human race would already be extinct.

Spindle was right. It's better they don't know.

RECYCLING DEATH

I was getting twice as many tests after I hijacked Spindle. I refused to cooperate. I was not allowed in the Preserve, not allowed to see Pivot and not one mention of Chute and Streeter, either. And, of course, no news about Spindle. Mom was more distant than ever.

They were punishing me, I think. But there was something else. Something had changed. When I felt angry, I saw something in their eyes. Something well-disguised, well-hidden, and controlled, but something nonetheless. They wouldn't admit to it, but it was there. I saw it. *Fear.*

I penetrated Spindle's database and that shouldn't have happened. They feared something about me. Maybe it was my potential. Maybe it was my unpredictability. Was I their obedient servant? Or a time bomb?

I would get a few hours of sleep and then they had me up again. I refused to cooperate. If they wanted me to play their Paladin games, then they needed to meet me half way. First, bring back Spindle. And he better be unharmed. But every day there was no Spindle. And every day I told them to go screw. My anger sometimes exploded in waves of heat. They could feel that. I know they could.

Eventually, they turned to their best weapon, Mom. She sat me down, gave me the cold facts: They'd keep testing whether I cooperated or not. They'd keep testing and testing. I wasn't going anywhere. I would become an old man inside this box and she wasn't bullshitting. But, she said, they will consider releasing Spindle if, and only if, I cooperated.

I held out some more, but in the end they won. Mom was right. I had no leverage. No matter how powerful I thought I was, all they needed to do was send in a guy like Pike and I'd be pissing in my pants again. And I had a feeling they had a lot of Pikes. That night I answered their questions. I read their thoughts, sliced time and did whatever they asked, just like a good boy. Whatever they wanted, I did it for what seemed weeks. I'd been inside so long I had no idea if it was Christmas or summer vacation. When I was tired, I slept. When I was hungry, I ate.

In between, they tested the hell out of me.

Spindle woke me one morning. He just walked into the room and the light came up. "Good morning, Master Socket!"

I rolled over, squinting.

"It is time to wake. I have wonderful news for you!"

Spindle opened a drawer embedded on the wall and brought pants, a shirt, underwear and socks to the bed. Neatly folded and neatly stacked.

"Spindle?" I said, shaking the sleep out of my head.

He turned his head, cocked it curiously. "There were adjustments made to my programming to account for your

100

extraordinary skills, but I have been cleared to interact with you again. Is that not wonderful?"

He pulled the sheet off the bed and helped me up. He brushed lint off my arms and held me by the shoulders. "I have come to inform you that your test results are complete. The Commander will meet with you tomorrow."

You're mad, Socket Greeny. You think you can stop time and believe human duplications are taking over the world. We'll need to chop your head off.

"According to my records, you have been sequestered inside the Garrison for twenty-five days. I thought you should come with me to the Graveyard this morning. It is our mechanical maintenance and manufacturing center. One of my duties is quality assurance. I can show you where your father worked. I think you will find it very interesting."

I think I sat there with the covers on my lap trying to decide if this was a dream. But there he was, the faceless one, all happy and glowing. He seemed more human than most people I'd met in the real world, but he was just a machine. He would hold no grudges for what happened. In fact, he was probably just happy to be back in the game. And I was, too. "I'll shower."

"Great!" He pumped his fist. "I will have breakfast waiting. Eggs, grits, bacon and poached salmon."

Spindle handed me a pair of earplugs before the leaper opened, strongly recommended I "insert them into my ear canals". We stepped into the Graveyard and the noise shook me. The plugs blotted out most of the sound. My hearing would be gone without the plugs.

Discarded machinery formed precarious walls on each side, loosely forming corridors. The ceiling was too high to see. The air was clogged with hovering platforms carrying parts and tools and equipment. Green servys rode on the platforms, steering them in every direction, giving the atmosphere the look of a well-organized hive.

Spindle waved for me to follow.

The corridors went in several directions. Openings in the spare-part walls revealed rooms without ceilings so platforms could drop in, deliver a broken something or haul a refurbished something away.

When we entered a room, the noise from outside stopped like there was a sound barrier. Each room was filled with fastidious green servys repairing, building or delivering. The first room manufactured cell-sized nanomechs, spewing them like molten clay on conveyor belts. It was packaged in boxes, barrels and vats and hauled off by an endless string of hovering platforms. A person supervised the room, standing behind a network of consoles, monitors and switches. Spindle walked along the conveyor belt, stopping to assess the products. He touched the clay. His face turned colors. He seemed satisfied, waved to the supervisor. The supervisor waved back.

"Did my father work here?" I asked before I fastened my ear plugs.

"Your father was Director of Operations."

"He never got his hands dirty?"

"On most days, he did not. However, he serviced one servy quite frequently." Spindle stood taller, his face brighter.

The clay-like nanomech stuff was shipped to the next room where it was piled onto a shiny platform. Some sort of current was infused into the blob that made it quake, then shimmer. It began to shape itself into a round oval, and then long jointed legs grew from it, four on each side, lifting the body off the ground like a giant daddy long leg spider with a glowing eyelight. It was ushered off to the side to make room for another blob.

"What's that?" I asked.

"That is a crawler. They monitor the Garrison outside the cliffs and accompany Paladins on certain missions."

Servys floated around the newborn crawler, working with the end of its legs. "Spiders are tremendous hunters," Spindle said. "They have the ability to move fluidly through any environment. They are excellent protectors."

Spindle visited the supervisor situated in the corner behind a wall of equipment. The supervisor guided us through the room, pointing out the various functions they tested: weapons, surveillance and the ability to rip most living things apart. The supervisor constantly looked at me, then looked away when I looked back. *Is that the Greeny kid?* I didn't hear him think that, it was written on his face.

At some point, we got to the weapons room. The supervisor sat at an island podium. She couldn't keep her eyes off me, and not in a good way. Spindle climbed onto the podium and I walked to the back of the room. At that point, I'd been looked over by every single supervisor. It was good to see that Paladins weren't immune to gossip. They were still human.

The servys weren't bothered by me. Most of the stuff was inner mechanisms and didn't resemble things too dangerous. Although, once assembled, they looked plenty lethal. It was the club-like handles in the back corner that got my attention. They were like the handle of a samurai sword missing the blade. They looked familiar, like the evolvers I used in virtualmode battles.

The servy gripped a white one. The handle unfolded inside-out, reshaped and fused to its arm. An iridescent dagger emerged. The servy diced a metal cube. There was no smoke, just thin slices of metal. The evolver dagger split in two, reformed into pinchers. The servy picked up a sliver of steel and squeezed it into a neat metal bowtie.

Evolvers were for real. After everything I'd seen, I still wouldn't have guessed that.

A bright light flashed somewhere far across the Graveyard. The floor shook. The flow of hovering traffic shifted, turning in the direction of the accident. Even Spindle and the floor advisor looked.

"There's been a change of plans, dear Socket." Broak was behind me, arms folded behind his back.

The air tightened. Automatically, I was on the balls of my feet, knees slightly bent. Broak strolled toward me, dragging his fingers over the bench. The servys backed away.

"What're you doing here?" I said.

"Regretfully, I have come to deliver a message."

The mental pressure tightened, spilling warmth into my chest. Broak manipulated my psyche, but he was no Pike. I tightened my mind, blocked his efforts.

"You see, dear Socket, I haven't had the opportunity to educate you. Allow me a moment, will you?"

"What?"

Perfect smile. "The Paladin Nation protects this world. We are the good guys who fight the bad, but we are more than that. You see, our aim is not just protecting the human race. Our primary business is perfecting it." He stopped, looked up. "Does this make sense?"

Of course not. "Sure," I said. "We're better than them, I get it. How about we discuss our global dominance on the tagghet field?" *Where I'll never go.*

"I know it is difficult to comprehend, but I am trying to help you understand the message, dear Socket. We're not better than ordinary humans, we're more evolved. We want the human race to become advanced, like us. Nature does the same, you see. Inferior species die off. Stronger, more adapted ones live on and multiply. We're helping the human race become stronger and more adapted for life in the universe."

"I get it."

"But every once in a while, even nature takes a wrong turn. It churns out the retarded and disfigured. And if their DNA is allowed to remain in the human gene pool, the race becomes less-equipped to survive. That is logical, wouldn't you agree?"

He rolled an evolver back and forth across the bench. His tone changed, words sharpened.

"The Paladin Nation has to be diligent, dear Socket. Sometimes we have to come to Nature's aid, to weed out her mistakes."

Most of the hovering traffic moved toward the thundering flashes that continued to shake the floor. The timeslicing spark glittered in my gut, moving on its own, trying to get my attention.

"Great, Broak," I said. "You're making total sense, I'm in total agreement with you, but I'm done with science class and not interested in taking it again. I'll catch you later."

"Pivot is a mistake," Broak said. He was a horrible listener. "But he is useful. You are also a mistake, dear Socket. We clearly don't know what you are, but you were not designed by gene scientists. You were a fluke of your father's tinkering. In other words, you are a mutation. There's a name for mutated DNA." He took another step. "It's called cancer."

"Step away, Broak." I clenched my fists.

"You see, you threaten me without understanding the message. You are unpredictable and unreasonable." He turned his head, daringly. "Do you think you can fight me and win? I was designed to fight. I know fourteen styles of hand-to-hand combat. I know every weapon in this room, intimately. It would be foolish to attack me."

"I can stop time. That's all I need."

His jaw muscles tensed and the pressure intensified, dumping adrenaline into my bloodstream. He could beat me in a straight-up fight, I'll give him that, but what good was that if he couldn't stop time?

Broak walked down the bench while my emotions boiled. He was getting inside me. I tried to fight the pressure, even opened my mind to read his, but it made things worse. I didn't know how to close myself from this mental attack. He was manipulating my emotions. He wants me pissed off.

Spindle was in the tower with the supervisor, still looking at whatever was flashing and rumbling. The tower elevated high above to get a better view.

I backed away from the bench, touched my cheek. "Spindle, come for me."

But he did not hear me. I took another step, every instinct telling me to run. I would *walk* away, not run. It was the smart thing. I turned—

"They murdered him, you realize," he said. "Your father."

My throat tightened.

"His workmanship was ghastly. Mechs leaked fluid, weapons jammed, cars whined. I'm sorry to report that your father was quite pathetic. So the Paladin Nation ordered his death."

Now I just couldn't walk away from that. If he wanted an ass beating, then all right. Let's talk.

"Murder seems quite drastic, I know," he said. "But do you know why they did such a thing?" He faked concern, drawing his eyebrows up like he cared. "His incompetence would eventually cost a Paladin his life, dear Socket. It sounds reprehensible to you, I realize, but if you weigh the balance of your father's life with that of a Paladin's, it was an easy decision, really. We had to weed out the weak and incompetent. For the good of the human race."

I was going to break his perfect freaking nose. "You're lying."

"You may check the records," he said. "It's all there."

I stopped inches from him. The timeslice spark crackled. "I don't know what your game is, *dear* Broak, but I'll give you one last chance to end it. Then I'm breaking your teeth."

"I told you, I'm simply here to deliver a message." He did not flinch. "I just want you to understand."

"I understand, all right. You don't have parents and you got some unconscious ax to grind but you don't know who to blame. So you pick me, the one with no dad, and open that wound to make yourself feel better. You're coping with subconscious pain. You're projecting it onto me. However the therapist wants to explain it to you, you need help. I suggest you get it before something goes wrong. Before you get dirty."

Broak was expressionless. He worked his lips but stopped the words. I was on the verge of timeslicing. He could feel it. The spark burned, tendrils of energy pulsing through my nervous system. My fingers dug deep into my palm.

He stepped back. The tension between us eased. He knew his limits. Whether he could kung fu or not, it wasn't going to do him any good when I froze his ass in time. He parted his lips and bit down, his teeth clicking together. Something shot between his lips and stung my neck. A pin-prick. I rubbed the left side of my neck, the spot already numb.

"What the hell did you just do?"

"I am sorry, dear Socket. The message has been delivered."

Something wiggled inside, bumped against my throat. I turned, pressed harder. My entire neck was numb.

Broak backed further away. I swung wild and fell to one knee. The wiggling went to the back of my neck and pierced my spine. I tried to scream but my throat was dead. My lips worked silently. I tapped my cheek, activated the nojakk, attempted to call Spindle. I couldn't make a sound.

I crawled on my knees, reaching for the tower, but Spindle was thirty feet above the ground.

Broak watched. I drooled a long string onto the floor. The wiggling sensation penetrated deeper. Numbness traveled down my spine. It reached the bottom and exploded. Fire erupted.

On my back. Colors bright. *Timeslicing.*

And I wasn't controlling it.

LULLABY

In timesliced silence, I lay still. I could see the ceiling now that the hovering platforms had thinned. It was a hundred feet above. It was blue. Like the sky. I could not feel the hard floor beneath me or the wiggling sensation in my neck. I couldn't move and I was alone. I'd die like that.

Just wish I could say goodbye to someone.

Unconsciousness came like a black fog, rolling in from above, eating up the remaining hovering platforms and gobbling up the walls. It came for me, creeping over my face. But something was moving within it. There was sound.

Pivot crawled over me and the black cloud scattered. He slid his fingers behind my head, probing a spot burning on my neck. I trembled, hoping he would get the message TO STOP DOING THAT!

He picked me up. The room spun.

In several blurry moves, we dropped into a dark, musty tunnel where the light was gray and the ceiling smooth. He put me down and his hair fell over his face. He listened like a morning bird, pressing his fingers on the back of my neck, again; this time harder and deeper. Like driving nails. Pain burned into my skull and down my spine. I was helpless to stop him. Unable to scream.

The source of pain was in my neck, branching like lightning, searing me from the inside, until Pivot pulled something out. I fell limp and relieved, taking tiny gulps of air. Pivot leaned against the wall, his knees pulled up. Something squirmed in his hand like a long crystalline horsehair.

[An accelerator.] His face was slick with sweat. *[Your energy centers are now attempting to prematurely bind.]*

"Broak did that." My teeth chattered.

[Yes.]

"Why?"

[Your awakening is failing.]

I pushed off the floor and winced. Small sparks shot down my back, crackling just under the skin. "I can still feel… things happening."

Pivot gently pushed me back down, placed his hand on my chest, turned his head and listened. He touched several spots. The Adam's apple in his throat bobbed up and down and a low hum vibrated through his hand. The humming was soft and numbing but the sparking pain fought back. I closed my eyes while Pivot moved his hand across my chest and hummed in different pitches. Sometimes loud. Sometimes soft. It tried to carry me off to a dreamy place, but jagged rips of pain yanked me back. He hummed louder to soften the blows. And then I would drift again.

Mmmmmmm. The sound travelled into my bones.

Warmth oozed inside and the pain receded.

Mmmmmmmmmmmmm.

I floated away and left the hurt in my skin. I saw Pivot hunched over my body with his hand on my chest and humming. I continued to float upwards and away. I tried to swim back but I was helpless. Despite the pain and agony back there, I wasn't ready to leave. Not yet. Please.

I went through the ceiling and into the ground above. I rose through the compacted soil and red streaks of iron. Roots appeared, branching out with little white tendrils, tiny hairs sucking moisture from the pore space. Higher still, there were more roots and insects feeding on them. I passed through it all and emerged above ground, into the sunlight.

A breeze rustled fallen leaves across the slab. Pivot was against the grimmet tree. Grimmets crawled down his arms and hung from his fingers. His lifted his head. A man walked up the stone slab with a bundle of blankets. He wore the uniform of a Paladin but his hair was long and face unshaven. *Father.*

He knelt next to Pivot and pulled the blankets open. A baby struggled in the light, his eyes clenched. He opened his toothless mouth and let loose a cry that woke every last grimmet hiding inside the tree's hollows. They shot from the branches and stormed overhead, casting an ominous shadow over the child.

Pivot turned his face up and grinned, his sightless eyes searching. While my father looked young, Pivot looked exactly the same. He touched the baby's chin, stroked his cheeks and touched his nose. The child stopped crying, wrapped his whole hand around Pivot's finger. Pivot's laugh came out like a hoarse bark.

The grimmets shifted and laughed, too. The child's gaze moved through the colorful cloud and the grimmets wrestled to get in front, sticking out their tongues, thumbing their noses for attention. Fights broke out. They whipped each other with their tails and pulled each other's ears. The baby squealed with delight. The grimmets crowded closer, making goo-goo and ga-ga sounds. Pivot waved them off.

"He's got my eyes," my father said. "And his chin's square, too. He's going to be strong. And independent."

That was me in the blankets. I hoping this was a dream and I wasn't watching my life pass before me.

My father placed the bundle in Pivot's arms. Suddenly, I was swaddled in the blankets. I'd become the baby. I could feel Pivot rocking me side to side. I felt his chest heave when he barked out laughter and the grimmets' wings beat the wind onto my face. I reached up for his face and caught a handful of hair. I pulled his face closer, felt his breath stream onto my cheeks. I felt so safe.

Pivot rubbed his nose against mine and cooed a lullaby, a sound humming deep inside his throat. It started with a single note, vibrating long and low, and then drifted up and down. He closed his eyes, moving his head to the rhythm of his wordless song. The grimmets joined in, their little voices humming a higher pitch.

Mmmmmmmmmmmmmm.

There was nowhere to go. Nothing to do.

MmmmmmMMMMMM.

The world was perfect in that moment.

Mmmmmmmm.

mmmm.

The ground quaked. I jerked into the rock and resurfaced. The tree was empty. Pivot was gone. My father was, too. A dust cloud swept over the rock carrying fallen leaves.

I went down again, hard this time. Past the insects, roots and rocks, and slammed into my skin like brick on brick. My teeth clamped. Something hardened like an iron fist in my groin. I convulsed. Another knot tightened in my stomach. My chest knotted. My throated constricted. Electricity ripped through me. Pivot's touch faded in the gloom.

112

The awakening had arrived.

I couldn't remember Pivot picking me up or how long he'd been carrying me. I could only see the tunnel fall away behind us. His legs were blurred below, moving inhumanly fast. The walls were flying by. My hair was plastered to my face, but I no longer felt fiery pain. I was just numb.

Where are you taking me?

[You must awaken.]

The tunnels were endless and all the same. Sometimes we took a left turn, sometimes a right. We passed through an archway outlined on the wall and dropped, then we went through another archway and dropped again. Vertigo churned my stomach. With each drop, the air turned colder and heavier. Pivot slowed, turned the last corner and put me on my feet. He held me up so I wouldn't fall.

I faced an archway at the end of a tunnel. The last stop.

Somewhere deep inside, I felt a quiver. Something I couldn't ignore. It was time to face my demons. "I'm scared, Pivot." My lips were fat. "I admit it."

He held me firm. *[Even heroes experience fear.]*

"I'm no hero."

The archway buzzed. I pushed back into Pivot. He held me tighter, then let go. The doorway drew me closer. My feet scuffed over the gritty floor. I reached back for Pivot but I was sucked through to the other side.

Agony returned.

The room was small and the walls etched with symbols. Blue light pulsed at the other end. BOOM-boom. BOOM-boom. Voices came from the light. They wanted me to come closer. I locked my knees but my right foot slid forward. I tightened up, leaned back, but the voices pulled. My left foot moved. Left, right, left I shuffled toward the light against my will. The voices were a jumbled crowd, talking among themselves, but the closer I got, the clearer they became.

[Who is it? This is unexpected. He is young... so young. This isn't right. Should he awaken? It's too late for him to turn back.]

They argued in circles, no voice sounding the same. Meanwhile, the room was volcanic. I was afraid to look down. *Is that my skin dripping?*

There were hundreds of voices now. Unseen fingers probed my body; feeling and studying. Deciding. Their minds penetrated me, looking through all the dark corners of my past. Memories opened, flipping too fast to recognize. They consumed the entire catalog of my life and all the intimate details, the ones I'd forgotten and the ones I wanted secret. I was completely exposed. Naked.

The voices stopped. The probing halted. In unison, they spoke one last word.

[Awaken.]

The blue light freed me from my skin. There were no walls. No ceiling or floor. I was somewhere in-between. The light was a ball the size of my head. Or maybe it was the size of a planet. There was nothing to compare. Maybe *I* was as big as a planet. The surface swirled blue and white. Liquidy. It pulsed, alive. I'd seen this before.

A virtualmode portal!

I reached for it. I don't know what I reached with, I didn't have hands, and I don't know why I did it. Something urged me to. I reached and reached, through endless space.

The voices chanted far away. They buzzed inside me, built tension until it felt more like humming than buzzing. The more I reached, the louder it felt and the tighter I became. The thinner I was until I felt so thin I didn't even exist.

There was a warm sensation when I merged with the portal. It filled me. Then I knew that I was not breaking, I was not thin, but I was full. I was everything, as if I was dissolving into the universe.

blip.

There was nothing. I think I screamed, but there was no pain. There was just nothing. I continued to dissolve into deep darkness until, for once, I felt complete peace. For once, I understood what this life was all about, and yet I couldn't say what it was. I could only be there. I could only experience it. *I understand.*

I faded into a dreamless sleep. Part of me hoped I would never have to go back to the skin, but I knew that wouldn't be. There was still so much to do. And so many people I couldn't leave behind.

UNFORGIVEN

It was sometime later, I woke. A dim light radiated under the bed. All kinds of things came out of the dark. Lookits hovered over me. Long mechanical arms extended from the walls, tending to a thick band wrapped around my left arm where tubes came out, one filled with blood, the other blue. I licked my lips. A lookit pressed against my mouth and squirted something.

They did their jobs like a surreal nightmare. Maybe it was the blue fluid pumping into my arm or I was just too tired to make sense. Or maybe the abnormal just seemed normal.

One of the mechanical arms touched my forehead and I was sleepy again. I woke a few times but no one was there. I dreamed that little creepy things crawled inside my head, went through my memories, putting everything back in place before I woke.

Then one day, I woke fresh and clear. The room was bright. I threw my legs over the bed and sat up. I touched my nojakk and asked for the date. Thursday. Three days had passed.

Broak tried to kill me.

I didn't ache or burn and none of my skin melted. I felt light and strong, my spine solid as a hundred year oak. Hot spots hummed along my back from my tail bone to the top of my head. And there were smells. Lots of them. The air was filled with thousands of distinctive scents. There were traces of people, servys, and food in the air and places they touched along the wall. There was a distinct tangy, steely scent. *Spindle.* And another scent mingled with it, another person was in the room with him. She smelled like jasmine. I sensed her on my wrist, the back of my hand, my shoulder. Mom was here.

I've awakened.

A tray extended from the wall with neatly folded clothes. I pulled the shirt off the pile, held it by the sleeves. It was dark, dark purple. The pants, too. I got dressed and the tray folded into the wall.

"You are feeling well?" Spindle came into the room.

I just looked at him, not knowing what to say. He had to know what happened, but you wouldn't know it by the way he walked in like any other morning. He put his hand on my chest, put his fingers to my neck. His face flashed multiple colors.

"Your vitals are perfect. You may follow me."

"Wait." My voice sounded different. Deeper, maybe. Richer. "Where are we going?"

"Your preliminary judgment." The colors on his face muted. "The Paladin Nation will decide your immediate future."

His skin was cooler than usual. His voice wasn't really Spindle-like, either. It was more business-like. More robot-like.

"What did they do to you?"

"Information classified."

"What?"

"I am not classified to discuss the case."

"What case?" I pulled him from the door. "Listen, Broak attacked me. He said some crazy shit about delivering a message, and then he shot this accelerator into my neck with his teeth..." Spindle's face contained no color. "Are you listening?"

He pulled his arm away. "We cannot be late."

The lights in the room dimmed. Spindle waited in the leaper, his shoulders thrown back and his head high. The leaper wobbled the moment I stepped inside. They did something to him, again. They stripped the Spindle out of him. Now he was just another servy. I started to say something, but he stepped through the door.

The room was enormous. Everyone in it wore the same color clothes as me. Mom was on the right next to the minty man, Walter Diggs. *Commander* Walter Diggs. His eyes were harder than the last time I met him, what seemed like a lifetime ago. Pike and two other minders with black wrap-around glasses were several yards in front of me. They were skinny waifs that were at least a foot taller than Pike and stood just off his shoulder a half-step behind him.

To the left, standing all alone, was Broak.

I clutched my fists and warm spots whirred along my spine. Time warped as the metaphorical spark glittered in my belly and I started after him. I had a message to deliver.

Spindle clutched my arm. "Control your actions, Master Socket. An act of violence will be dealt with severely." His face darkened. "Crawler guards are on alert."

I yanked my arm but his grip tightened. Broak stared ahead, unblinking. He didn't plan on me surviving. The minders went through my memories; they would see what he said. They would see him spitting the accelerator. He would get what he deserved.

"Please step forward." Spindle pointed at a circle glowing on the floor.

The spongy floor squeezed between my toes. Mom and the Commander stood with their arms locked behind their backs. Her lips were thin and her eyes red. The Commander had a soldier's unmoving expression.

The room rumbled and sections of the floor rose up behind the minders, forming a horseshoe wall encircling us all. The room turned brown, the floor hard marble, and the ceiling sky blue. Men and women appeared at the top of the wall, like a panel of judges, from the chest up. Soldiers' expressions.

"Hearing 24489 of Socket Pablo Greeny," a woman's voice rang through the room, "is now in session. Evidence mined from Socket Pablo Greeny's memory has been presented to the committee. Witnesses and the accused are present."

A big man with slumping shoulders sat directly above the minders at the top of the wall. He looked around the committee and cleared his throat. "Socket Greeny." His voice boomed. "Do you know why you are here?"

I shook my head.

"I see." He looked down at notes or something. The rest of the committee kept hard looks coming. "You have accessed an awakening portal without authorization."

I moved my mouth, searched for words, then found them. "Um, Your... Honor?"

"You may address me as Authority." His deep set eyes hid under the shadow of his protruding eyebrows.

"Your Authority, I don't know what this is all about. Broak approached me, initiated my awakening with an accelerator, which was like this squiggly wire he shot out of his mouth and went right in my neck." They stared, no one saying a thing. "Look, I know this sounds crazy, your star pupil over there attacking me out of jealousy and all, but it happened. Just check my memories, it's all there."

The Authority held up his hand. "Broak is not on trial. It is you, Socket Greeny, that we are here to judge. I'll confirm that you understand why you are here and we can continue."

"Wait, he's not on trial? How can... are you kidding? He tried to kill me!"

He held up his hand again and I stiffened under his psychic pressure. He looked around the circle and each member of the committee returned his knowing glance.

"Each of these members is projecting from around the world, so let me get on without further interruption. Your preliminary results are exceptional, demonstrating the highest potential the Paladin Nation has ever recorded. Including the young man to your left." He nodded to Broak. "You have very promising timeslicing skills and have demonstrated superb psychic aptitude. For a cadet, that is quite impressive, especially at your age. And while you might claim cadet Broak attacked you out of jealousy, the minders have probed both your minds sufficiently and shown no evidence to support your claims."

"Impossible."

The Authority grimaced, on the verge of emotion. "We're not here to play games, Socket Greeny. The memories mined from you were distorted by your premature awakening. Many of them were indecipherable, colored with hallucinations. Broak's memories were clear and accurate and have been confirmed by security. You two had an argument. Broak instigated the altercation and has been reprimanded for his behavior. However, the fact remains the argument incited your awakening. Provoked or not, this is of concern. All of this has been confirmed by the minders."

"Him?" I pointed at Pike.

"The minders monitor each other. There was no deception on the part of Pike, I can assure you. There is enough psychic power in this room to keep him from concealing anything from us."

"This isn't fair!" I looked around for support, but there were only soldiers looking ahead, letting me dangle. Mom quivered, her jaws grinding, but she held still. "That isn't what happened, Authority! He attacked me! Check the records. He spit an accelerator through his teeth—"

"Enough!"

I slammed my fists into my legs, careful not to step out of the circle. This couldn't be happening. He's getting away with it. I glared at Broak, standing at attention. I reached with my mind. Invisible psychic tentacles wrapped around his head. I squeezed. Broak shook, his face twitching in pain, until an icy lance of psychic energy cut through me. I almost fell. The minders hadn't moved, but had immobilized me physically and mentally. One last cold wave squeezed my brain and I could breathe again.

"Authority?" Pike said.

"Continue."

"I'm willing to excuse cadet Socket's insolence due to his ignorance and youth." Pike's left eyebrow twitched.

"Noted." The Authority leaned forward, furrowed his wild eyebrows. "No more interruptions. The real issue, Socket Greeny, isn't the unauthorized awakening or the intrusion. It is your stability."

The atmosphere tightened. The air moved in waves. I stood straight, drawing air to purge the scraping discomfort of Pike's mind against mine.

"Your father was feral, which means he developed Paladin powers outside the breeding program. Therefore, you will face greater scrutiny because of your potential instability. The fact is, there are many Paladins that do not want you awakened, regardless of your potential, because you were not bred. Do you understand what I am saying?"

I nodded, efficiently.

This pleased the Authority. His lower lip plumped out and looked to his notes, once again. "Let me officially recognize that Socket Greeny prematurely entered the awakening phase. While this does not prove instability, it is suspect. He infiltrated the awakening portal, a most sacred source of power hidden deep within the Garrison, to complete the awakening—"

"He could've died!" Mom finally broke, stormed in front of me. "He did what any Paladin should do! He assessed the situation and responded accordingly! And you ignore the evidence that cadet Broak incited this premature awakening and you condemn my son for saving his own life!"

The Authority stuck out his chin, his brows setting his eyes deeper in their pockets. The Commander stepped to Mom's side, put his arms around her, nodded to the Authority and ushered her back. Her cheeks flamed.

"I WILL NOT TOLERATE ONE MORE EPISODE OF IMPUDENCE!" the Authority said with the booming voice, shaking the walls on which he sat. "The next outburst will be dealt with severely, Commander Diggs. Is that understood?"

The Commander nodded once. Mom resumed the pose, hands behind her back and head down, quaking. Pike's expression softened with a curl at the corner of his mouth.

The Authority took a deep breath. "This matter is not an easy decision. The committee understands that cadet Broak was involved in a confrontation. We also know that Socket Greeny was *taken* from the Graveyard. This person who took you there will be held responsible, just as you are."

"Pivot?" I said, barely above a whisper.

"He will be judged when found."

Found?

"However, the committee has voted, 8 to 7, for a continuance to further investigate the matter," the Authority said. "In the meantime, your abilities will be clamped. You will not be able to timeslice or exercise psychic ability. You will reenter society. The clamp will prevent you from discussing Paladin matters and will remain in place until final judgment is rendered. Do you understand this, Socket Greeny?"

"You're going to make me normal?"

"For a time."

Like normal was punishment.

"Very well," the Authority said. "If there is no more from the committee?" He looked around and got cold stares in return. "Then hearing 24489 will conclude. You will be summoned for final judgment in four weeks. Please be escorted to receive the clamp." The Authority nodded to me. "Good day."

The wall collapsed into the floor, taking the images of the Authority and his companions with it. Pike and Broak quickly went to a leaper on the other side of the room. Not until they were gone did the glowing circle disappear and I could move. I tried to speak, but nothing intelligible came out. Mom put her arm around me. I tensed.

The Commander still had his hands behind his back. "You have a lot of questions, but for now there is business at hand. While you were recovering, we lobbied for a continuance to further investigate Broak. If what you believe is true, there is much to understand."

What I *believe*. Even he thought I was cracked.

He patted my shoulder, but not so much like everything would be all right. More like *hang in there, kid.*

"But—"

"Socket, you truly don't understand the impact you're having on the Paladin Nation," he said. "When you display your kind of potential, you make enemies as fast as allies. Penetrating Spindle's database caused a lot of concern, but this awakening…" He paused. "I want you clamped so

123

there are no problems while we sort some things out. It's the only way."

Mom squeezed me, again. "I'll be with you very soon."

I could feel her emotionally disconnect. I had always felt that hollow craving for her, the missing element of a mother, but now that I was awakened it was painfully present. No escaping the dull pang of watching her leave with the Commander.

Or just leaving.

Spindle guided me to the leaper. He was stiffer, consciously picking each leg up and putting it down. There was no sway at the hips. His eyelight was fixed on the destination. He stepped in the leaper and did an about-face fresh out of boot camp.

"Where're we going?" I said.

"We will go to the infirmary to have the clamp installed. Your mother will meet you there to take you home."

"Home?"

"Yes."

"They're letting me go home?"

He didn't answer because he was a program and my question didn't make sense to a program. Spindle would've answered, but not that hollow shell. I could sense his optical gear viewing me as another human, just a task to complete. Once he was done, he would move on to the next thing on his list. And that was to put a clamp inside me.

CLAMPDOWN

We entered an infirmary with a sterile table in the center. A hood of lamps hovered over it. Three rotund servys waited. The one in the center was red and larger than the others.

"Lay face down on the platform," Spindle said.

I swore I wouldn't do it again, but I *reached out* to read him. It got him reprogrammed the last time, but what was there to lose? That wasn't him standing there.

When I moved my mind this time, it seemed as effortless as lifting my arm. I could take his memories like plucking apples. The circuit fluid flowed with a steady rhythm, not the BUM-bum of a heart but the mechanical efficiency of a pump. I sensed a fresh set of criterion burned into his procedural code. He had recently been reprogrammed, but this time there was a dimness surrounding his circuits. They shut down his heart processor, the thing that made him Spindle. It was what made him curious.

Spindle shut down my psychic intrusion, kicking me back to my own skin. "Lay on the table."

"What're they going to do?"

"The medical mech will install a suppression clamp."

An appendage grew from the center of the red servy. It looked more like a talon than it did a hand. It held a c-shaped ring.

"The suppression clamp," Spindle said, "will fit between the third and fourth vertebra."

"You're going to put that thing inside me?"

"You will not feel it. The servys will render you unconscious for the nine-minute surgery."

The servy's fingers were sharp as scalpels. My fingers twitched. The awakening stripped away the mystery of timeslicing. I saw inside myself, how it all worked. I clenched my hands to timeslice, but that's not really what did it. The fingers were just a crutch, what really triggered the timeslice was a signal from my brain, altering the metabolism throughout my body. I could turn it on or off with a thought.

And the clamp would take that away.

I needed a minute. I had to talk with the Commander, there had to be another way. I would stay in the Preserve, if that's what they wanted. Maybe I could find Pivot. I didn't have to go home, as long as they didn't put that thing in my neck.

The surface of the red servy glittered like a magical orb. A halo engulfed all three of them as I timesliced. Spindle had his hand raised. Maybe he anticipated what I was about to do. I just wanted out of the room. I could figure out how to operate that leaper. All I had to do was *reach* inside its circuit panel.

Legs emerged from the leaper door, multi-jointed with sharpened tips. A crawler stepped into the room, bright and glistening in the timesliced light. A red eyelight burned on the front, directed at me.

They're watching.

I let go of time and the crawler vanished, returning to its post, waiting to see if I was foolish enough to try it again. Spindle stood at the corner of the table.

I scanned the room for a weapon. Fighting was a ridiculous thought, sure, but I had to exhaust every possibility before I gave in to what was about to go down.

"Lay down."

"You're going to have to make me," I said.

Spindle did not move. Instead, ten more servys entered the room. There was barely space to move, but I would stomp them until I couldn't stomp anymore, if that's what it took. But it didn't take the servys to disarm me. It was a scent. *Jasmine.* I could sense her before she entered the room.

"I know it's hard," Mom said, touching my arm. "But there is no choice. Without the clamp, the Authority and his committee will not agree to a continuance. They want to send you home to keep you out of the Garrison. They want you disarmed and far away. It is the only way, Socket. It is the only choice we have."

She pushed the hair behind her ear. Despite the pale look, she was strong. I would fight every Paladin before doing what they wanted, but it only took a look from her, and a gentle touch, to change my mind and to fill the empty ache.

The table reformed to fit my body. My face fit in the opening and didn't restrict my breathing.

"The medical servy is going to place nighter gear on the back of your head," Spindle said. "It will only take a moment."

Mom held my hand. The medical servy pushed my hair around and slid something cold against my scalp.

Her hand was warm.

The nighter gear whined.

My head vibrated. My teeth, lips, and tongue became numb. And then, like a switch, it was night.

I was sitting up. I think.

"I'm going to stay with Socket tomorrow," Mom was saying. "I'll make the meetings by projection. I've already forwarded apologies that I can't return in person, but I think they will understand. If all goes well, I'll be back the next day."

She was right in front of me, digging through her briefcase. Spindle was next to her, standing at full attention. His face was dull.

My blood was like syrup. I was afraid to turn my head. It might fall off.

On a floating chair.

In a hallway.

Mom wasn't standing, she was walking.

We were just in a room. Now we were going through a doorway. We entered the dank stalactite parking garage. Mom's car was at the bottom of the steps. Servys stood at the open doors. One of them took Mom's briefcase and loaded it into the back seat. Appendages grew from the ones next to me and took my arms. Their fingers were soft and tacky. They helped me inside the car and shut the door. When I looked out, Spindle was already gone.

The car banked sharply to the left and we flew through the wall and over the boulder-strewn field. A crescent moon was fading in the sky as the sun was about an hour from rising. The dashboard was illuminated with instruments, casting an orange glow on Mom's face, accentuating the lines pulling her eyes. We drove without lights.

"Spindle had to be washed out." Mom pretended to steer. "The Authority wanted him deactivated for his involvement in the incident. They suspect he somehow helped you escape the Graveyard through an unmarked exit. They think he had something to do with Pivot's disappearance, too. The Commander had to compromise with the Authority. Spindle's personality was deactivated."

I rubbed my neck, felt the raised line where the clamp was surgically implanted. The seat sensed my discomfort, wrapped tightly against my neck and applied heat. Live oaks blotted the moon from view in a black sky. We were already in South Carolina. I couldn't remember going through the wormhole.

"I don't like this." I touched my lips. They didn't feel right. "My voice sounds weird. This doesn't feel like my skin."

"Your body is adjusting. It'll take a few hours for your nervous system to accept the limitations of the clamp. Soon enough, you'll feel just like you did before all this started."

"Why'd you let them do this to me?"

"Many Paladins aren't in favor of your awakening. The clamp bought us time to change some minds."

"You *want* me to be a Paladin?"

She sighed. "If they vote to permanently disable your awakening, you won't be the same. You'll be alive." She wouldn't look at me. "Just not the same."

Just like Spindle.

She took her hand from the steering wheel and plunged her thumb into the moody. I was tempted to pull it away from her and make room for my thumb. I'd try anything to take this deadness away. If the moody helped, then a big fat thank-you goes out to the drug companies. The Paladins had me. *Check.*

"That's illegal," I said. "They can't operate on people against their will. There are human rights that protect people from that."

"No one even knows we exist."

She said 'we'. She's one of them.

"You have to understand, they can't let someone with the ability to timeslice back into the general public. If a cadet is considered unsuitable, unstable, or incapable, they will alter the nervous system to squelch his or her abilities."

"I didn't ask for this."

"No one does."

"You're one of them." I said it like a right hook.

Mom took a moment to dig her thumb in deeper. Her next breath trembled.

"You have no idea what lurks in the world, what kinds of danger threaten our very existence every single second. As reprehensible as the Paladins seem, they're our only hope. I don't expect you to understand."

We passed an exit that connected to a northbound Interstate, lights flashing. The road was open and long. If we went north without stopping, we could be a thousand miles away by daybreak.

"We can't run," Mom said. "They'd find us within the hour."

And checkmate.

We turned onto the highway heading home. Few cars were in the way. It was close to the middle of the night. Mom let go of the wheel and let the car drive in auto-pilot.

"Broak said they assassinated Dad."

"Your father was respected in the Paladin Nation. If there was even a hint of foul play, the Commander would've investigated the accident until the day he died. You're father was in an accident. Broak was merely taunting you."

I tried to *reach* out to see if she was telling the truth. The clamp slammed against the bottom of my brain. I moaned.

"Don't try that," she said, taking my hand. "Any attempt to do *something*, it will hurt."

I was normal now. I had no *power*. It was what I wanted, to be normal, but now that I had a taste of the awakening, normal didn't seem all that normal. I wasn't sensing Mom's jasmine-flavored energy anymore.

Off the Interstate, Mom took the car out of auto-pilot. We turned left, waited at a stoplight, then made the last right home. Almost eight months had passed. The azaleas were in full bloom in front of our house. Our porch was lit. We silently coasted up to the driveway. Someone was on our front steps. I threw the door open before the car stopped, ran across the grass and crashed into Chute. She crushed me in her embrace, weeping into my shoulder, her chest heaving against mine.

"I didn't think you were coming back." I could barely understand her. "I didn't think I'd see you again."

My heart was clutching. Suddenly, I realized just how much I missed her.

"Glad you're back," Streeter said. He didn't hug me. He sort of punched my shoulder while Chute squeezed me until I couldn't breathe. "It hasn't been the same without you."

"Come inside," Mom said on her way to the door. "It's too late to stay out here."

Chute and Streeter stayed the night. We talked until 3:00 that morning. Never once did they ask where I'd been. Maybe Mom prepped them; those questions were off limit. Or maybe they didn't care, they were just glad to see me. Maybe both.

Chute slept in my bed. Streeter and I crashed on the couches. For once, Mom slept in her room. It didn't take long to fall asleep. I was glad to be home.

III

Every self-aware intelligence eventually asks the question:
Who am I?
There is a yearning to know the answer, to find out what
we are and where we fit in. Do we matter?

BLEED

There was some discussion whether I should go back to school. Truth be told, Mom didn't care either way. In fact, I think she wanted me to stay home. In my entire life, there had never been a morning I woke up excited about going to school. Not one. I didn't care about what field trips we were taking or movies we were watching, I'd just rather do something else. But when I was home alone and everyone else was at school, what else was I going to do?

I slacked off around the house for a week. It took that long just to feel halfway normal with the thing in my neck. I could feel it when I turned a certain way or thought about something that had to do with Paladins. Once, I imagined telling Streeter and Chute everything and the damn thing about knocked me out. Most of the time it just wiggled and vibrated like something crawling under my skin. I couldn't stop thinking about it, so I had to get out of the house. I packed my book bag and caught the bus in late April.

Two freshmen were whispering in front of me. Occasionally, they looked around the cafeteria, pretended to search for a friend as an excuse to look at me. I pretended not to notice. They went back to whispering. The line moved forward. One of them grabbed a lunch tray first; the other had to run to catch up. They looked back, one last time, not bothering to whisper anymore.

There are rumors about where you went, Streeter had told me. Yeah, I heard the rumors, too; whispered behind hands when I walked down the hall and in the locker room when they didn't know I was there. I was under CIA investigation and got locked up in juvenile detention. I lost my mind in the virtualmode journey and had a nice long stay in a psych ward. I joined a secret cult worshipping technology and was building a space craft in a secret hideaway. That wasn't too far off, really.

Streeter waited for me to say something about the freshmen. When I didn't, he stared at the menu with an unspoken question left on his tongue. Every day he wanted to ask the question, but he didn't. Where *have* you been? He never asked, but every day he came a little closer.

I stepped up to the window. "Um, give me a three, eleven and a twenty-two."

A metal tray rolled out. Applesauce, cheesecake and chicken spilling over the sides and mixing together. The servys would never let that happen. I followed Streeter into the cafeteria. Chute was at a table by herself, wearing a purple jersey. An *athletic* jersey.

"Nice shirt," I said.

"Thanks," she said. "You were on vacation when I got it."

Vacation. That was what she called it. I went on vacation for eight months, just didn't bring back any pictures.

Chute smoothed the front of her jersey, showing off the holographic lightning bolt across the front, illuminating our mascot: a fox stomping through the swamp. In the time I was gone, tagghet had moved into the high school system and teams were formed and a stadium built. Spindle wasn't kidding; the sport was exploding. Chute told me how her dad nearly knocked over a light when she made the team. The more she talked, the more her freckles crunched in her dimples. If I could feel her energy, it would be vibrant and tingly. I imagined it smelled orangey. But the clamp stopped all that. It was an ever-vigilant fairy that stole the words from my mouth when I even thought about saying something that might reveal the existence of Paladins or dupes. Instead of sitting on my shoulder, this fairy was buried in my neck and turned me into a robot. *Follow orders, Socket. Or else.*

"I wish I could see you more," Chute said. "We've been doing two-a-day practices for the last week with the game so close. They're talking about a huge crowd, too." She took a deep breath. "I'm getting nervous."

I cut another piece of chicken and looked away. When she talked about tagghet, the memory of Broak bludgeoning a servy popped up. He was smiling when he did it, cold and perfect. If I let the memory linger, the clamp throbbed.

I rubbed my neck.

"They'll stop whispering, Socket," she said. "Just give it some time."

She thought I was bothered by the rumors. People seated near us were talking and I hadn't even noticed. I grunted, chewed my food. Honestly, I didn't give a rat's ass what they thought, but I let Chute believe it bothered me. It kept her from asking what was really on my mind. Streeter was too busy eating to notice anything.

"You coming to my practice tonight?" she asked.

"I want to. Really, I do. But there're so many people there. I'm not really into crowds right now."

"You're going to have to get used to it, sooner or later."

"I vote for later."

"I'll save a seat for you in the stands, have the coach post lookits around to keep people away."

"Oh, that'll work," Streeter mumbled, food spilling out of his mouth. "No one will wonder who the royal prince is with the king's guard. The lookits will just point at him."

"What if I give you guys tagger uniforms?" she said. "You can stand on the sidelines, blend right in."

"Or you can dig us a hole at center pitch, cover it with a trap door," I said. "We can watch you with a periscope."

We laughed. Streeter pounded the table. Everyone looked at us again, wondering what was so funny this time. *Look, the freak is laughing.* It didn't stop me. I pictured a bunker with a manhole cover over the top. I could push it up and look with one eye over the edge. Were they thinking the same thing? Before I could stop myself, I *reached* for their thoughts to see. The clamp slammed against my spine.

I held my neck and moaned. They asked if I was all right. I said yeah, it was just a migraine. Streeter wondered how a migraine gets in your neck. Chute pried my fingers away to see what I was hiding. I wanted her to stop, but didn't want to put up too much of a fight.

"Where'd you get that?" she asked, touching the thin red line on my neck.

"It's nothing."

Streeter stood up. "It looks like you got operated on."

"It's nothing." I spooned some applesauce off the tray to look normal, but my hand shook.

Chute traced the line with her finger. It felt good. I wanted to tell them everything, but I couldn't go there. I couldn't even tell them I couldn't tell them. I wanted them to know what I really was. I wanted them to know there were Paladins hiding in mountains with amazing technology and a bona fide jungle. I wanted to tell Chute about the grimmets and Streeter about nanotechnology. And Spindle! They would love him (if he were back to normal). And what if Streeter knew about the dupes? *Dupes? In the skin?* He'd piss all over himself.

Streeter and Chute knew everything about me. Now, my entire life was a lie. I wanted to be closer to them, but the secrets built a wall around me. They could feel it, too. They knew I was keeping something from them. I was even more alone than ever and I never thought that was possible. If only I could tell them—*pppssslllptttt.*

A wad of pizza splattered on my forehead.

"Bull's-eye!"

Several tables over an uber-punk group of bleeders – boys and girls, all with black eyeliner – stood to get a look. They were a bunch of freaking wannabe vampires. The only thing that separated them from the goths was two spots of fake blood on their necks. Plus, they were giant assholes. The biggest of the bunch weighed nearly three hundred pounds and had a freshly shaved head that shined under the cafeteria lights. He used to play football in middle school, but he got kicked off the team for beating up one of the assistant coaches.

"Freak," he said, deeply.

The table shook in my grip. The clamp quivered, grinding against my spine, and not because I wanted to read his mind. No. I fought the urge to show the fat ass bleeder just how freaky I was. The clamp made sure I didn't.

The entire cafeteria watched, not even trying to hide it. The bleeders were after someone. Better yet, they were going after the freak! It's a main event! Fat bleeder drew his lips back, exposed tobacco-stained teeth and blew the imaginary smoke from his imaginary finger-gun. *Bull's-*

eye. But he wasn't finished. The crowd was behind him now. They all wanted to see it go to the next level, but I was just sitting there with a two-handed grip on the table. He reached for another chunk of pizza. If I was going to be a willing target, then he didn't need an invitation to take another shot.

The table legs chattered on the floor.

Chute snatched up her water bottle. Her wind-up was tight, the release quick. The plastic bottle flew on a straight line, end over end, and hit that fat make-up-wearing dickweed so square in the forehead that it bounced straight back. He shuffled sort of cross-eyed.

The laughter paused.

Silence drifted from table to table. Laughing at me was one thing, but laughing at this guy could shorten your life. But the laughter started again, this time with the bleeders around him. They laughed right at him. And then the cafeteria followed right along. The dumb bastard rubbed his head and looked at his fingers to see if he was bleeding. Then he swatted the bottle off the table and kicked a chair. The crowd cleared a path between us. Round one was going to be a bloodbath.

I still couldn't let go. The timeslicing spark flitted in my belly, aching to be clutched. But if I take the spark, the clamp knocks me out. The table quaked so violently that the trays were moving over the surface. All I could do was watch him stomp toward us, fists at his side. He was going to roll me like a garbage truck.

Chute stood in front of me. Streeter slid his chair out and stood up, too. He was a half-step behind Chute, but he was up. He wouldn't be anything more than a stepping stone in fatty's march to mutilation, but he might slow him down half a second. I closed my eyes, breathing deeply and calmly, hoping to get the clamp under control. At the very least, I could stand up with Chute. I'd fight the guy straight up, no Paladin powers needed; I just needed the clamp to SHUT THE HELL UP!

Chairs slid behind us. Fat bleeder stopped. Lacrosse players and tagghet players, united, surrounded our table. The 'crossers were bigger, stronger and meaner than the taggers, but there were enough of both to stall lardass and his troupe of fake bloodsuckers. Chute was out in front.

Streeter leaned over. "You want to get up?"

Fat bleeder wasn't a fan of a fair fight, as long as he was on the winning side. I could sense the simple math burning in his brain as he calculated the odds. They were outnumbered five to one. There wasn't a chance in hell, but there was also a lot of snickering going on behind him. Either anger got the best of him or he was really shitty at math because he came at us, fists up. His crew was behind him, coming like a band of theatre misfits, climbing over tables and chairs, stepping on food. The 'crossers stiffened. The taggers crouched.

"BACK TO YOUR SEATS!" Lookits dropped in like hornets, their eyelights spinning. "Go back to your seats before authorities are called."

The bleeders stopped a few feet away. Their hate shimmered like summer heat.

"An assault will be treated as a criminal offense." A lookit went to eye level with the fat one. "You have a previous record. Do not make this mistake."

The moments ticked long, the crowd silently hoping he'd do it anyway, knowing security would be there any second. He finally opened his hands and surrendered. If he could breathe fire, he would've roasted that shiny ball. He swatted at it, instead. The lookit dodged, effortlessly, repositioned near the ceiling.

"Another day," he said to no one in particular.

He went back to his table, his crew in tow. He slapped one of them in the mouth. The others stayed out of reach, still snickering. Security arrived. They walked through the crowd and had a little chat with the bleeders. The cafeteria went back to the daily chatter and whispering and staring.

"Oh, man, that was close." Streeter collapsed in his chair. "I thought we were dead meat."

"You didn't have to do that, Chute." I wiped the pizza off with a napkin. "I can take care of myself."

"You expect me to sit there and watch?"

"That guy is twice your size. What were you going to do, chew on his kneecap?"

"If that's what it takes."

The 'crossers and taggers went back to their seats. Some of them slapped Chute on the back. They weren't standing up for me.

"You're one of them," I said. "Congratulations."

"No, Socket, I'm just me. I play tagghet, but I'm just me." She grabbed her tray and stood. "You know, a simple thanks would be enough."

She walked off. The bleeders watched, whispering.

"Why are you complaining?" Streeter said. "She just saved our lives, man."

I finished cleaning my forehead, dropped the napkin. I let out a long sigh. Things were so messed up.

"You need to say you're sorry," Streeter said.

He was right. I needed to apologize. I'm sorry the shadow turned me into a freak. I'm sorry there are Paladins out there and dupes threatening to kill every last one of us. I'm sorry my mom doesn't come home. I'm sorry there's a clamp in my neck that beats the shit out of me whenever I want to say something real.

I'm sorry that nothing will ever be the same.

After school, I made my way down a shortcut past the lacrosse field where they practiced in shorts and helmets, past the empty baseball field to the brand new tagghet field. It was oval and green with three sides hemmed in by live oaks. Large bleachers flanked each side with a smattering of fans.

I hid in the trees close enough to watch. The team flew around the field flipping the tag back and forth, bouncing it off the ground or throwing it across the field. The coach barked plays from the sideline. I couldn't see their faces, but I could see the player with red braids swinging from under her helmet. She soared across center field on the jetter faster than anyone and caught a long pass in full stride, faking the defender with a backhand and spinning around to sling it into the scoring cube. The fans stomped the bleachers, cheering.

I tapped my nojakk. "Nice shot."

Chute looked around while her teammates patted her on the back. She tapped her nojakk, asked where I was. I told her. She looked in my direction. I stayed in the trees and watched the entire practice, chiming in with a comment whenever she did something outstanding just to let her know I was there. Whenever she scored, she looked my way.

When I got home, there were several messages. I didn't answer them. Streeter was sure to be calling, wondering why I didn't meet him in Buxbee's virtualmode lab after school. That night, I was on my bed, tossing a roll of socks at the ceiling when Mom called. *I'll be home late, but I will be home. You'll have to order out.* I told her not to stay too late.

A delivery man dropped off an order of Chinese food. I ate it on my bed and fell asleep without brushing my teeth and a half-box of fried rice on my bed. When I woke in the morning, there was a message on my nojakk. Mom's room was empty. She never made it home. Her message was an apology.

Something unexpected came up.

IN THE PIT

Mom came home twice that week. Both nights she collapsed on the couch and fell asleep. I made dinner and cleaned up. By morning, her bed was made. She was gone.

She was back to her old ways. She rarely came home. She checked in on the nojakk every evening, told me to order out. Sometimes I didn't take her calls. We were having the same conversation, so what's the point? And we were back to the mother-son relationship with few words and no feelings. I stayed up as late as I wanted and watched movies. I stopped brushing my teeth, altogether.

The days at school went by uneventfully. I seemed to be smarter than before. I never forgot a thing my teachers said. While everyone was taking mad notes, I just listened and nailed the exams. Sometimes, I think I understood the subjects better than the teachers. Everything was just so logical. I suppose the clamp couldn't stop me from thinking.

I blended back into the normal crowd at school. People stopped staring. Even the bleeders forgot about me, throwing food at other people. Everything was back to the old days. I went to my hiding spot every day after school to watch Chute practice. I wanted to see her, sure, but more than that I had to stay out of the house. The longer I sat around by myself, the more I started thinking. The slightest Paladin-related thought turned into a headache that could last for hours. But if there was a distraction, it was easier not to think, but then after awhile I would wonder why I wasn't thinking and remember the clamp.

Headache.

The nights were the worst. Sleep came in small chunks. The clamp even monitored what few dreams I had, and anything that crossed the line pounded my ass. I spent hours going through meditative breathing exercises to empty my mind. I couldn't even think about when the Authority was going to rule. It should've happened weeks ago. All I could do was stay in the moment. But the moments were getting longer.

Streeter slept over every other night, and that helped. We stayed up late watching movies. I was careful not to catch any news reports. It was hard enough to keep from wondering who may or may not be a duplicate at school; I didn't need to be reminded about it on the TV. I caught the news once by accident and watched it long enough to see protesters fighting for the right of virtualmode duplication. There had to be a few in that crowd, or maybe all of them. One was a frizzy-headed dude that got plowed by the cops when he threw something. Did it hurt when the cops planted his face in the street and cuffed his hands behind his back? Could they control pain? Were they like computers?

The clamp taught me not to think about that.

I wanted it out. If that meant moving my shit into the mountain and never seeing Streeter and Chute again, I'd do it. This was no way to live. But even when I asked Mom when they would decide, she wouldn't tell me what was taking so long.

But the whole world was about to find out.

It was the week before finals. There was a pep rally for the inaugural tagghet season at the end of school but no one seemed to care except for the taggers wearing their jerseys to class. There was more talk about football and that was five months away. The tagghet season was only going to be two months long and go through the summer so it wouldn't interfere with more important sports, like lacrosse, baseball, basketball, football, soccer, tennis and softball. Tagghet seemed to rank just above tetherball for the time being.

It was the period just before the rally. I went to virtualmode studies in the Pit, a steep, circular auditorium with a domed ceiling. Buxbee was down at the center table. I made my way to the front where Streeter was waiting with his transporters in hand. I left the seat empty between us. Chute's seat. She wasn't in class very often. She'd been doing the assignments in the evening when she had time. I sat in her seat once before and Streeter insisted I move over. I thought maybe he thought it was gay if we sat too close. Maybe he did, but I think he missed her. He wouldn't admit it.

Buxbee was a round man with a bald head and a horseshoe of hair around the outside. He tended to plump his bottom lip when he thought. He had a finger in one ear talking on his nojakk, his brows pinched together.

"You promised you'd launch today." Streeter handed me a pair of transporters.

I had gone virtualmode only once since I got back and it was weird. Just as my awareness was pulled from my skin, there was some back and forth chatter between the transporters and the clamp like they were telling secrets about me. It didn't get any better once I was in my sim. I started skipping virtualmode lab after that. Headaches, I said. Then I'd go to the nurse and she'd let me lay in a dark room until my migraine settled. Turned out that wasn't much better because I'd start thinking and end up with a real migraine.

Streeter watched me trace the edges of the transporters. He sighed super loud. Twice. He already had one empty seat next to him. He didn't want two. He once grumbled that I'd changed, that he wanted it to be like it was before I went on my vacation. *Ditto that, brother.*

"All right, all right," I said. "I'm going, like I said."

Class was running ten minutes late. Buxbee was still chatting on the nojakk with fingers in both ears to hear over the class. We tried to launch into virtualmode, but the transporters weren't active. Streeter was already being accused of crashing the school's portal.

"Attention!" Buxbee held up both hands. "I have an announcement. Everyone, I have an announcement." He walked around the center with his arms up like he was signaling touchdown. After one trip around, he dropped his tired arms. His bottom lip plumped out and tension tightened his forehead. "Virtualmode is down for the day."

He didn't bother talking over the moans and groans and Streeter getting blamed for it. This was the last week of school when everyone had a free pass to virtualmode anywhere and the school had one of the best portals in South Carolina. The experience was ten times richer than any home connection or any commercial connection in the tri-county area. Now Buxbee was telling them it was a no go. "Don't do this to us, Mr. Buxbee," someone wailed.

When it was quiet enough for someone to ask why things were shut down and it was quiet enough for Buxbee to speak, he explained. "This is not a local blackout," he said. "Virtualmode has been shutdown *globally*."

Another uproar, this time with a trace of curiosity mixed in. People were looking back and forth like they just heard the front end of a juicy rumor. Buxbee held out his hands, calming the class.

"I've uploaded the final assignment to your accounts. You can complete it when it's back up."

When, why and what happened? All those questions were met by Buxbee's plumped lip and a shake of the head. When it was clear he didn't have the answers or wasn't willing to part with them, everyone broke out the laptops and tablets to look at the Internet on a screen. Buxbee was back on his nojakk with a finger in his ear. Everyone was getting updates and I didn't want to hear it. The clamp was beginning to throb.

Streeter pulled out a collapsible touchpad and stretched it open on his lap. Three-dimensional images projected on the surface. He activated the sound on our nojakks. A global virtualmode blackout was the same as closing all the airports. It didn't take but a second to find the news. The reports claimed that a third of users were unable to launch into virtualmode that morning at approximately 6:32. At first, it was a minor inconvenience. Connections were typically re-established within minutes. Typically, a portal facility experienced a small anomaly, something like a sunspot that was easily corrected. But then complaints started coming in from all over the world, threatening transportation and financial trading. At 7:29, the entire virtualmode grid went dark.

"That's never happened before," Streeter said.

I was rubbing the ache in my neck. I should've looked away. Knowing more wasn't going to help, it was only going to make the banging between my vertebrae louder.

But I couldn't look away. And I couldn't help thinking. I let the thoughts come. *A third of virtualmode users? Did the Paladins block the world from virtualmode? And if they did, why? It had to have something to do with the dupes. Maybe they were beginning to distinguish the difference between people launching onto virtualmode from the... dupes? But why shut down virtualmode?*

The clamp slammed into that thought. I clenched my teeth. But I kept watching.

At 9:55 that morning, there were reports of federal testing of employees at a portal facility. Agents would not comment on what they were testing for since drug and euphoria-gear tests were made public. The testing was not met kindly by the employees and arrests were made at an independent portal facility where riot police were called. They charged through the doors into a warehouse of glowing portals.

The scientists and laborers didn't look surprised. In fact, they looked ready for them. They had weapons. Forty-two police were killed. There were a lot of dead workers, too, but the footage was censored even though police were required to fully disclose all public news footage. However, the report claimed all lookits stopped operating in the warehouse like they'd been shut off.

I was holding the back of my neck with both hands. I needed to get some air, needed to get out and clear out the thoughts, but the last scene caught my attention. I had to grit my teeth just a little longer. I had to make sure what I saw was right.

"Rewind that," I said.

Streeter wasn't sure what I was looking for. I turned the view on his lap and expanded a close-up on a white-coated scientist at the very back of the facility when the riot police made their entrance, before the bullets started flying. We both leaned closer to make sure what we were seeing. It was low resolution and pixilated. But I was right.

"That's impossible," Streeter said. "That's instant death."

Yeah, it was impossible. For real humans.

The scientist had his sleeves rolled up. His arms were plunged up to the elbows inside an open portal. That amount of energy was enough to vaporize flesh from a human being, but that wasn't a human doing it. The dupe in the white coat was glowing blue. *What the hell is going on?*

I ran up the steps. I don't remember getting to the doors. Everything was blotted out by the bright light of pain.

VACATION

I couldn't stop the thoughts. They needed to be assembled before I could forget them. I needed to make some sense out of what had come up at the Paladin Nation, what kept Mom from coming home, what kept the Authority's decision in limbo while I held my neck with both hands to keep it from exploding.

The Paladins were raiding portal facilities to test for duplicates. The Paladin Nation must've made police forces around the world aware that something was up, somehow tricked them to help flush out the enemy without them knowing what they were really looking for. But why did that guy in the warehouse have his arms plugging into the portal? Did the dupes need access to virtualmode to survive?

"Socket?" Streeter said. "Are you all right?"

I must've slid down the wall. I was sitting on the floor in the hallway with my knees against my chest. I held out my hand, told him to give me a minute. I managed to turn the mind-scrambling pain into a dull reminder with several deep breaths. The thoughts clamored for attention but I didn't give them a place in my mind to cling and felt them dissolve.

Streeter helped me up. "Let's get out of here," he said. "I've been helping Buxbee install security updates on the school's virtualmode portal. Let's go down to his lab."

The empty hall was much less stuffy. A slight breeze cooled my sweaty face. I concentrated on walking, breathing and holding the clamp down.

"Are you sure you're all right?" he asked.

I muttered something and kept moving. I was seeing spots but things were clearer. I couldn't manage a conversation. But Streeter filled the awkward silence with a question that started the avalanche all over.

"What'd you think they're testing for?"

The clamp thumped a warning. *Don't go there.* "I can't talk about it," I spit out.

"Can't talk about what?"

"Never mind," I said. "I can't talk about it."

"But why can't you—"

"Goddamnit!" I grabbed the back of my neck. "Just stop, will you?"

"All right, all right," he said. A teacher looked up from his desk as we passed his class. A lookit showed up a minute later. Streeter flashed a pass to Buxbee's lab and it buzzed away. We went down the hall quietly.

"So what's wrong with your neck?"

"Stop asking questions!"

"What the hell is wrong with you, man? I'm sick of you snapping at me all the time. Ever since you got back from your *vacation* you hardly talk and you never do a goddamn thing. You half-baked on some euphoria gear or something?"

"Do I look like I'm having a good time?"

"You look sick. In the head."

"I'm going home."

"That's great." Streeter stopped in the middle of the hall. "Go home then, forget about me."

"It's not like that."

"Then what?"

I couldn't let go of my neck. The lookits returned and told us to shut up or we were going to the office instead of Buxbee's lab.

"Just forget it," Streeter finally said. "Go home and do whatever you do. Clearly, you got more important things to do."

"I can't talk about some things, but that's just the way it is, Streeter. There are things you just can't know about." *Jesus Christ, who does that sound like?*

He looked at my neck. I still hadn't let go. He tapped his teeth together; the question he'd been holding back for weeks filled his mouth. He could hold it no longer.

"Where'd you go on vacation, Socket?"

"Streeter... don't."

The floor sloshed up and down like a one-winged airplane. I started toward the exit, pulling my head down to steady the bucking clamp.

"Your mom told us to let you work it out on your own, but all I see you do is go home." He stopped me before I reached the exit. "Where'd you go, Socket?"

My brain was going to hemorrhage. *Bump, bump, bump.* "I can't do this."

He called after me. Said he was sorry, I think. He didn't mean it.

I got on a bus and lay in the back seat. It wasn't the right bus, but it went toward town. I got off downtown, caught a taxi home, lay down in that seat, too.

The pain shot down my spine with each thump. It wasn't letting up this time. I pushed too far. Something was wrong. The cabby adjusted the rear view mirror; his eyes flickered from the road to me. *You okay, kid?* Somehow, I convinced him I was.

I ran in the house and went through breathing exercises. I concentrated on each breath and cleared my mind. No thoughts. Just this moment. But the clamp still rattled. The thoughts still came.

They're torturing me.

I tapped my cheek. "Mom."

The nojakk ticked. She wasn't answering.

"Mom," I said again, tapping my cheek. "Mom. Mom. MOM!"

"*Socket,*" she said. "*I'm in a meeting.*"

"I can't do this. This thing in my neck has gone off. It's killing me. You got to get it out, I can't take it."

I sniffed back tears. There was a long silence. I thought we lost connection. Maybe she was leaving the meeting.

"*There's nothing I can do, Socket,*" she said. "*Go through some breathing—*"

"WHAT GOOD ARE YOU?" The pain took control. "You let them do this to me then tell me to just do some breathing exercises! What kind of mom does that, huh? What kind of mom leaves their son like that? WHAT'S WRONG WITH YOU?"

The room looked blurry; I couldn't wipe the tears fast enough. Snot was dripping.

"*Why don't you get the moody out of my top drawer, it'll take off the emotional edge.*"

"I don't want a goddamn moody! I want this... this thing out of me. I want all of this to go away. I don't want to be one of you people! Let Broak... the rest of those...

154

freaks... let them save the world. I want out. I want to be normal, AND THIS ISN'T NORMAL!"

The words jumbled together in a muddy string of confusion. I collapsed on the couch, muttering into the cushion. I thought we had lost connection again. I figured I was alone. Again.

"I know this is hard." Her voice was soft, but firm enough to make me listen. *"It takes a strong person to do it, Socket. You are that person. I know you want to quit, but sometimes life doesn't ask for your permission to act. Life demands. And when that demand falls on you, it does so for a reason."*

I bit on my lip.

"I can't say any more than that, Socket, because quite honestly I don't know any more. I only know the world is lucky to have you. I see so much strength in you. I know you can't see it, but I can. You have to trust me. Trust what I see in you. One day, you will see it, too."

She didn't sound like she was on a mission this time. She sounded more like someone helping me with an impossible task the only way she could. Like a mother.

"Get some rest. The clamp will be out soon. I promise."

Somehow, the pain receded. It still hurt, but it was washed in sorrow. I fell asleep on the couch. The clamp thumped in the distance, kept me from dreaming. I went in and out of sleep, fighting to stay under. I pulled a blanket over me, hid my head, took my sweat-soaked shirt off. I managed to sleep until a hand gently touched my shoulder.

"Have you eaten?" Mom asked.

My eyes were puffy. "No."

"Go take a shower. I'll make dinner."

The pots and pans rattled in the kitchen. The hot water washed down my neck, the heat seeping through, dissolving the pressure. By the time I dressed, food was on the table. Mom sat across from me. We didn't talk much, but we ate together. She cleaned up. By the end of the night, the clamp's presence was a whisper.

Mom stayed home the next day. It was weird, seeing her play mother. She was probably good at it once upon a time. It took her a while to find the utensils and food. She made eggs for breakfast. By mid-morning, she did breathing exercises with me. She talked me through them, helped me focus. She talked a lot about the present moment and one breath at a time. The clamp became tolerable.

I slept through the afternoon. Mom took a meeting in her bedroom by projection. The house looked orderly. That night she made dinner. We ate quietly, then cleaned up together. She washed dishes by hand. I dried and put them away.

"How'd you become one of them?" I asked.

"Your father and I studied genetic engineering in college. We took jobs with an engineering firm that turned out to be a recruiting agency for the Paladin Nation." She rinsed a plate and handed it to me. "If I knew what I was getting into…"

I flinched, excepting the clamp to react to the word *Paladin*, but it lay quiet. We washed some more, then I chanced a reply. "You wouldn't do it?"

She mulled that question over. She started cleaning the sink and left the question alone. She didn't know the answer.

"How'd Dad become one of them if he wasn't in the breeding program?"

"Your father was a genetic engineer. He worked on splicing Paladin abilities into adults."

"He did it on himself?"

She pinched her lips together on the bitter memory. She nodded, then said, "The method didn't work, though. The ability wouldn't fully awaken and after a while the powers faded. His program showed great potential but was discontinued until further notice."

"And that's why I'm like this?"

"We think so."

"So it worked."

She started wiping the refrigerator. Decided not to answer that one, too.

After clean up, the clamp reminded me it was there, again. Maybe it realized, in retrospect, that the conversation about my dad was really about the Paladins.

Mom sat with me. We breathed in.

Breathed out.

I made it through another night. By morning, she was gone. *There is an urgent meeting,* her message said. *I'll call you later.*

Life resumed, a little less painfully.

A little less empty.

WATCHDOGS

The sun was setting at the first ever South Carolina game of tagghet. I wore a dark hoodie because the weather was cooler than usual. Everyone at that game would remember what they were wearing. Small details, like what you're wearing and where you were, are easy to remember at life-altering events.

The parking lot was mostly full. Must've been more people than the school expected because there was only one security guard and he was busy with an eighteen-wheeler that was obviously lost and now plugging up the parking lot.

I found a spot at the top of the visitor's bleachers, upper left hand corner, right where Streeter was going to meet me. We talked the night before through nojakk. We didn't say much. I couldn't tell if he was pissed or sorry.

The benches were firm but slightly molded. This sport had money. The scoreboards had video screens bigger than they needed to be. The disposable programs had imbedded videos that explained the rules of tagghet and how they could get started on their own tagghet career. *You-know-who* had to be funding this through various businesses. They seemed to be fond of the sport. Or maybe it was their way of introducing technological advancements to the rest of us.

The oval field was empty. The seats were filling up and the anticipation to see flying discs was in everyone's conversation. The little kids started jumping up and down on their seats when the scoreboard lit up. The first tagger rode onto the field to cheers from both sides of the field. He banked left and the person behind him went right. They alternated until the entire home team was on the field, the grass swooshing in their wake. Everyone was on their feet.

They formed a circle, riding clockwise, and slung a red tag back and forth. The lightweight sticks flexed with each one-handed toss, expertly fired across the rotating circle. The curved end of the stick had some sort of magnetic impulse that grabbed the tag. I couldn't recognize anyone, except for the one with red braids dangling from under the tear-shaped helmet. Chute caught a pass on the short hop and tossed it to the far side of the circle with a sharp backhanded flip.

If I could *reach* out, I could feel her nervous energy. *Taste* its jagged frequency. Maybe I could help soothe her nerves, she was always nervous… but I couldn't think that way.

The visiting team rode onto their end of the field and the people around me cheered. That's when I noticed Streeter lumbering up the steps. He turned sideways and excused himself down to the empty space next to me. People were still standing around us.

He pulled a bag of popcorn from his jacket and filled his mouth. "Been here long?"

"Not long."

He stuffed two more handfuls in his mouth, chewing loudly. We sat there and watched the field, but since everyone was standing there wasn't much to see.

"So what've you been up to?" I asked.

"Been helping Buxbee with the security updates. Global virtualmode is back online but authorities aren't letting independent portals open until updates are operational. There must be serious."

"The updates are taking longer than I thought, but we're almost done." More popcorn fell on his lap than went in his mouth. "I'd ask what you've been doing," he said, "but that didn't work out so well last time."

"Right," I said. "Nothing personal."

"Why would I take it personal? You wanted to punch me in the face."

"I wish I could explain…"

"But you can't." He picked at a kernel stuck between his front teeth. "You know, I've been thinking. If you can't tell me what's going on, then it must be a big deal."

I grunted. Half-laughed.

"And that one of these days, you'll tell me everything."

I'd tell him everything right there, on the spot. He would never know how much it was killing me to withhold from him. He was always the first to know my secrets. Streeter and Chute were the only ones that kept me from feeling all alone in the world. Sitting next to him with all those secrets, I didn't want it that way. *But when life demands, you answer.*

I held out my hand. "You'll be the first one I tell."

He smiled, his lips glistening with butter, and slapped my hand. Then I reached into the bag and grabbed a handful. Then we watched us some tagghet.

The teams huddled along the sidelines. They had their hands in the middle, chanting and jumping. Captains from each team met at center pitch. The coaches went with them. "Welcome to the soon-to-be-most-popular sport in the world... *TAGGHET*!" a voice rang across the field. "Where your Charleston Rapid Foxes take on the Columbia Bolters. Now, introducing the inaugural season please welcome, Coach King!"

Coach King was the lacrosse coach, too. He walked onto the field wearing his purple shorts and socks pulled up. He held up both hands and our players slapped them as he made his way to center pitch. He said something like: Great sport, some of the best talent you'll ever see, we were going to win the state championship like we do in every other sport. And if anyone wanted to learn how to tag, training sessions were available.

"And now!" he shouted. "Your Rapid Foxes!"

The scoreboard projected an image of each tagger, live from the field, as he called their names. Some kept the yellow visor down, others retracted it into the helmet.

"And starting at left lancer, and the only female tagger to start varsity... Chute!"

Only he said *Shhhoooooooooot.*

It could've been my imagination, but it sounded like she got more cheers than anyone else. She was the only girl out there. Chute cruised in a small circle near center pitch mumbling. I couldn't see her lips, but that's what she does when she gets nervous.

"She almost quit, you know," Streeter said.

"Quit what?"

"Tagghet. She was so worried after you left she couldn't focus. Your mom told us you were all right, you were just having some medical tests, but after a month, Chute wasn't herself. Your mom wasn't coming home and we weren't hearing anything at all. She was a wreck, said she was quitting."

"Why would she quit?"

"She didn't feel right having fun while you were…" He glanced at me. "While you were probably *not* having fun."

I watched her floating in a tight circle with the stick yoked over her shoulders, muttering. I knew she was glad to see me come back, but we didn't talk much about the time in-between.

"How was that going to help, I told her," Streeter said. "I mean, you weren't coming home any sooner if she sat at home and twisted her hair." He fished the unpopped kernels from the bag. "You know what I mean?"

"So you talked her into staying?"

"She loves the game, Socket. It was just stupid to quit. Besides, she needed something to keep her mind off of you."

"She never told me that."

"Mmmm, imagine that, someone keeping a secret."

I could see her taking deep breaths. Something was delaying the start. I wanted so badly to take away her discomfort, but all I could do was watch.

Finally, a lookit dangled the tag over center pitch. A player from each team squared off under it, shook hands. Not one person was sitting. It got loud. Numbers counted down on the scoreboard to zero.

The tag dropped.

The centers chopped at it. The Bolters pulled the tag away and set up an offensive formation on their side of the field while our team retreated. Chute hovered near their cube. The Bolters attacked and the Rapid Foxes looked confused, running into each other. The Bolters threaded a pass between the two defenders. Two passes later, one of them rode up the dome, caught a pass and rifled a shot into the scoring cube.

GOAL!

"That was easy," I said.

Streeter didn't hear me. I didn't even hear me because the kid who scored was related to the lady in front of us. She curled her fingers and screamed his name like she'd been stabbed.

"The team is breaking up," Streeter said.

"They just started, give them a chance."

"I mean us." He patted his chest. "You, me and Chute. *Our* team. We're falling apart."

I shook my head and watched the teams regroup. I didn't know what he meant.

"We used to do everything together," he said. "Now Chute's out there and you're… doing whatever you're doing."

"It's not a vacation, Streeter. Believe me, I wish I never left."

It was the closest I came to telling him something. The clamp didn't budge.

The teams squared off at center pitch again. This time the lookit dropped the tag to our team. Our center took it behind three blockers and set up a play. Chute flared out to the left.

Streeter wasn't watching. He was thinking. I gently elbowed him, reminded him that he was the most popular virtualmoder at school. Reminded him he was globally ranked. I mean, the school trusted him to patch the security codes into the portal. I reminded him that he would never be alone, if that's what he was thinking.

He nodded, but he wasn't listening.

Our team lost the tag. The visiting crowd cheered.

"Remember when we were kids and you and Chute would come over?" Streeter said. "We'd enter Level V tournaments when we were Level I. Remember what we named our team?"

"Watchdogs," I said. "And we got slaughtered."

"You would spend the night and once my grandparents were asleep, we'd virtualmode to another tournament."

"And get slaughtered again."

"Remember the time we planted a data bomb in the principal's account and froze it for a week?"

"*You* planted it."

He looked up at the moon hanging just above the school. "I'm going to miss all that."

The Bolters looked to score again but lost control of the tag. The visiting fans groaned.

"You'll invent something and become filthy rich," I said. "Maybe Chute will become a professional tagger. It doesn't matter, none of that changes the team, Streeter. We're the original Watchdogs."

"What about you?" he asked. "What're you going to be doing?"

"I'm sure I'll be around." *I might disappear, but I'll be around.*

Now I had the distant look. What if the clamp got removed and I returned to the Garrison for good. What would Mom tell them then? *He went on vacation. Forever.*

"She's open." Streeter jerked my sweatshirt.

Chute slipped past the defensive line. Her teammate had the tag. He got around a defender, darted to the sideline and zipped a sharp pass across the center pitch. Chute caught it fully extended.

We stood on our seats.

Chute lost her balance for a moment and a defender intercepted her on the way to the dome. Chute leaned heavily to the left, pulled the jetter almost on its side to stop. She juked left. Right. The defender lunged after the tag dangling from the end of her stick. Chute spun, got behind him. Her stick flexed to the limit and the tag came off like a bullet, just a blur that straight-lined into the center of the green cube.

GOAL!

The home bleachers were about to come crashing down under the cheering stomps. Streeter and I were the only ones cheering on our side of the field. Chute's face appeared on the scoreboard, strands of red hair plastered to her cheeks. She was mauled by her teammates.

For a moment, I forgot about the clamp. I forgot about the Paladins and the uncertainties and all the unanswered questions. I wanted to run down there and hug her. I wanted to drag Streeter with me and we'd squeeze her until her head popped off. I wanted it to be just another night in our lives, just like it was when we were Watchdogs.

"Socket?" Streeter said.

He tugged at the back of my sweatshirt. I was busy screaming Chute's name through my hand-megaphone, hoping she'd hear me. I thought about nojakking her but there was no way she had it turned on.

"Socket!"

I shrugged my shoulder. It felt like he had his arm around me. "Dude, what are you doing?"

"What the hell is that?"

"What's what?"

He looked at my opposite shoulder. He didn't have his arm around me. A long red tail curled under my chin. Rudder poked his head around my hood, his golden eyes looking into mine. I quickly stuffed him inside my hoodie. No one but Streeter seemed to notice.

I looked around, completely suspicious, then pulled the collar out and whispered, "What're you doing here?"

Rudder purred against my chest. Warmth radiated deep inside.

"Did I just see that?" Streeter said.

I sneaked a few glances around, then opened my sweatshirt for Streeter to look inside. It might've looked creepy, but no one was watching. I started to introduce them, but knew the clamp would start thumping. "Ummm... this is... one of the things I can't talk about."

Streeter stared. Rudder stared back. Blinked. Waved his little fingers. Streeter waved back. He looked like he was waving to a… well, waving to a little dragon in my sweatshirt. The lady in front of us turned around. I smiled back until she was uncomfortable enough to look away. Rudder crawled around my side, tickling my ribs up to my neck. I tried to grab him.

"What's it doing?" Streeter said.

"I don't know."

I reached into my hood to pull him off, but he scampered up to the back of my neck, lay flat against the thin red line, and purred louder. The vibrations sank into the clamp. The ever present ache, low and dull, faded. I almost drooled. I bent over and hid my face. I think Streeter said something. The vibrations got stronger, warmer and deeper. Rudder suctioned tightly to my skin.

There was a sharp energy beside me. Clear and clean. *Streeter. I'm feeling Streeter!* I braced myself for the clamp to buck, but it lay still beneath Rudder. I opened my mind to the ebb and flow of the crowd's collective energy. The joy and frustration, cheer and anger. The essence of hundreds of people mingled through me.

A scene unfolded in my mind. Mom went to the grimmet tree. Rudder came to her, as if he was waiting for her. The other grimmets sat on the branches and watched her walk off with him on her shoulder. She took him outside the Garrison. At the base of the cliff, she held him up.

"Free him," she said.

Rudder shot from her hands, smudging the air red like a streaking star.

I opened my eyes. The game was still on. The air was thick. There was a charge in it, an unnatural tension, like the moments before lightning strikes.

[Pivot came to her.] Rudder's thought was as clear as if he'd spoken it. *[He told her to release you from the clamp.]*

Pivot's back? Is he all right? Do the Paladins know?

[He told her They are coming.]
Who?
[You must get your friend.]
Streeter?
[The girl.]
Who are They?!

He returned to working on the clamp. *[You must hurry.]*

It was nearly halftime. Chute was flying across the center pitch, her stick up high calling for the tag.

They were coming. That could mean only one thing. The duplicates were going to fight back.

No one would forget this night.

ARACHNOPHOBIC

I could feel them. The duplicates were here, at the game. I stood up and looked over the crowd. I sniffed the air like a bloodhound. There was a scent, a feeling, but I couldn't locate it. The clamp wasn't completely deactivated; Rudder was still working. *Faster. Go faster, Rudder.*

"Sit down, clown," someone said behind me.

Streeter stood next to me. "What's going on?"

There were hundreds of people here. I sensed all their individual essences intermingle, how their emotions ebbed and flowed, what kind of thoughts they were having. Somewhere out there was a different flavor. Something that tasted plastic-like, something fake. *Duplicated.*

"Hey, the both of you," someone shouted. "We can't see the game."

The lady in front of us turned around. It wasn't her. I could feel her pulse quicken when I looked at, looked *into* her. I could taste her essence. The same for the people around us. Even the guy that was standing up and reaching over a row to snatch my hood to get my attention. He was real.

I pushed Streeter to the side and we forced our way to the isle without waiting for people to move. One guy told us to get some goddamn manners. I stopped on the steps. The fake feeling was stronger. Streeter was apologizing behind me when I saw it. The eighteen-wheel truck was still in the parking lot. It was rocking side to side. Something was getting ready to escape.

I took the steps three at a time. "STOP! GET EVERYONE OUT OF THE BLEACHERS!"

No one could hear me except the people around me that figured another high school kid lost the battle with drugs. I leaped off the bottom step and crashed on the track that circled the field, then I jumped the fence onto the soft grass. I sprinted onto the field, waving my arms. "CLEAR OUT THE BLEACHERS!" I screamed at the home crowd.

Whistles were blowing. Assistant coaches were already after me. The taggers slowed down to watch the madman sprint over center field. I kept ahead of my pursuit, made it to the other sidelines, leaping over the other fence. I could hear them laughing. The security guard was nowhere to be found. Every lookit was on my tail beaming their eyelight at me but they weren't going to do shit.

I made it around the home bleachers and no one was listening, but people got out of my way. There were half a dozen men after me, some of them fans just trying to keep the crazy off the field.

"EVACUATE THE BLEACHERS!"

The parking lot was fifty yards away. The truck was going side to side so violently that the tires were lifting off the ground. People were taking notice and I felt a shift in

169

mood. Some already were moving in the other direction. But I couldn't stop. I had to let them all see where I was going. They all had to see that something was about to happen.

A man appeared in front me. Just appeared. His clothes snug and dark blue. Another two men blipped into existence next to him, their hair cut tight. Their expressions hard. *Paladins.*

I stopped. My pursuit stopped, too. They saw the Paladins materialize from a timeslice. I understood they had temporarily stopped time but the others didn't. They were trying to process how these hard men just appeared and what they were doing with the spikes in their hands. Why were they sticking them into the ground and why was a yellow laser beaming straight into the dark sky?

"CLEAR THE AREA!" I pushed past the gathering crowd and their blank stares. I clenched my hand, searching for a grip on a timeslice but couldn't get there. "SOMETHING'S IN THE TRU—"

The explosion was bright.

Then it was dark.

It sounded like a high pitch.

I couldn't remember what I was going to do. It was something. Something urgent.

The darkness took form. First it was just that some blobs were darker than others. Then there were lighter colors flapping through the darkness. It looked like snow drifting out of the sky. I had that feeling like I needed to wake up for school or something. A blurry face popped up like a puppet.

"We got to go!" Streeter's voice was far away.

I could taste the tang of blood. The fluttering white things, they were debris: paper and cups and popcorn bags. Panic crawled over me. The atmosphere tensed. Streeter pulled me up. "Are you all right?"

170

I touched my head. The bleachers were partially shattered. People were running. They were screaming. I saw people pulling limp bodies from the wreckage. I saw some bodies that were just laying there.

"We got to go, get up." Streeter pulled some more. "Get up, man. WE GOT TO GO!"

I got up and the world was wobbling. The Paladins were setting more spikes that looked like yellow bars circling the flaming truck. Beyond that, the school walls had crumbled. Half of the dome over the Pit was missing. With each spike and yellow bar, the heat from the roaring fire cooled. They were sealing off the site, protecting the civilians. They only had six up when the thing blew again. I could hardly feel the second explosion except through the ground. What would the place look like if they had got here a minute late? Would there be anything left?

Maybe they weren't protecting the public. Maybe they were here to catch something.

Streeter led me onto the field. I stumbled after him. People ran past. Half a dozen taggers lay in the grass. Chute was one of them. I pushed Streeter off and ran, sliding into her on my knees, wrapping her in my arms. A blue knot was on her forehead, blood trickling between her eyes.

She touched my lip. "You're hurt, Socket."

"We have to get out of here," I said. "Can you stand?"

She saw Streeter behind me. "What's happening?"

The ground shook from a muted explosion, this one not as intense. The yellow bars had contained most of the sound as well as the impact. "Socket." Streeter pawed at my arm. "Socket, Socket... you got to... you got to see this."

The dome had completely collapsed, and fire erupted from it, licking the sky. Something was poking out of the burning trailer. It looked like a tree branch, but it wasn't burning. It was growing out of the flames, red-hot and pointing up, and then it bent on a hinge as it cooled. It grew longer and bent at another hinge several feet below the first. More of them emerged, bending at angles until they were long enough to reach the ground and lift an oval body from the carnage. The giant daddy long leg spider stepped out of the flames, its glowing body cooling.

The crawlers had come with the Paladins. They would save us. But something wasn't right. Why were they coming from the truck?

The Paladins locked the last of the spikes in the ground, sealing in the heat and sound from our side of the parking lot. Their evolver weapons unfolded around their hands, glowing blue, then engulfed them in protective bubbles just as the crawler reared back. The bottom of the crawler's body opened. I could hear it through the ground, the sound the thing let loose was shrill and deafening. It vibrated through the bottom of my feet. The Paladins faltered but the shields held.

Chute latched onto my sleeve. "Who are those people?"

I wanted to tell her they were the good guys but I was watching them spread out while a second set of legs emerged from the flames. The crawler backed up like a mother protecting her newborn in a burning nest as the Paladins set to attack. I think Streeter or Chute might've asked what those things were. I thought I knew what they were, but the Paladins were attacking them. They were sent by an enemy.

The duplicates are coming.

PILLARS

It was a scene from a movie. People were running. Screams and cries and hysteria soaked the air. Bodies were all around. Some were dead. Sirens could be heard in the distance and the first of many emergency vehicles started down the road. And there were still only three Paladins. Three! Where were the rest of them?

That's what didn't make sense. A disaster like this and the entire Paladin Nation should be here treating people. Instead, there were three of them and they were barely holding their own against the duplicated crawlers oozing non-stop from the burning wreckage. The fire flickered red, yellow and blue as it burped out one spider after another. The agents sliced and diced them but some escaped and made for the giant hole in the Pit.

The spot on my neck warmed. I touched Rudder still working on the clamp. As he deactivated it, knowledge seeped from him as our minds intermingled. It came to me not as thoughts but more like a stream of memories that imbedded themselves in me, as if he were melting into me. I saw what he saw, knew what he knew. And then I understood.

The duplicates were attacking worldwide.

While the duplicates had dissolved into the general population, Paladins discovered they needed to stay in touch with virtualmode as if it was some sort of life force. They didn't know exactly how or why they needed to periodically get back into virtualmode, they just knew that if they cut them off they would die like weeds without roots. Paladins installed worldwide code that kept duplicates from logging into virtualmode. After that, the Paladin Nation went about flushing the duplicates out of hiding, even alerting public authorities about illegal virtualmode activity. It was only a matter of time before they starved. And the duplicates knew this. They were cornered.

It was fight or die. They chose to fight.

The crawlers were doing the duplicates dirty work. They'd sent them to seek out access to virtualmode. Schools, cafes and businesses across the planet were being attacked simultaneously, hoping one of them could circumvent the security patches, get to the inside of virtualmode and unlock it for the rest of them. The duplicates were waiting for the life-giving taste of virtualmode. They held their last breath, hoping.

Paladins didn't see the wide-scale attack coming. Of course not. They didn't have their fortuneteller anymore. Pivot was still missing. But Pivot saw. And that's why he sent Rudder to free me. He needed me for a reason. He needed me in the fight.

"They're after the portal," I muttered.

Streeter and Chute were staring at me with mouths open. I forgot to tell them all the details, but what was I

174

going to tell them? They were witness to it all. I just pointed over my shoulder and said, "That's what I couldn't talk about."

Streeter was sort of nodding, watching the ongoing fight, the sounds muffled by the pillars. Chute was staring at me, though. I could feel her fear, taste it like a bitterness at the back of my throat, a rotten energy eating at her stomach. She was freaked by the death and destruction, and she was wondering what I was. She felt guilty for fearing I would leave her again despite the misery all around. I took her hand. Her energy flowed down inside me and I opened to let it flow back into her, mingling with the fear that rolled inside her. *[It's all right.]*

I didn't force the thought into her mind. I didn't make her believe it. I just laid it out for her to see. She blinked. The smile of relief didn't show on her face, but I felt it rise inside her.

"Why are those things climbing into the Pit?" Streeter said.

"I think they're accessing the portal."

"But... that's like twenty feet below ground and encased in hardened steel. They can't..."

His thoughts trailed off. Maybe he realized he was watching spiders climb the wall and that reality was doing a 180 on him.

For some reason, those things were going after the portal. And the Paladins desperately wanted to stop them. "Is there any way to access the security patch?" I asked Streeter. He looked at me, but his glassy eyes were unfocused. "Streeter, how can I get to the portal security?"

His lips quivered but his thoughts were a mess. I needed answers quicker than that. I started for the pillars.

"You're not going in there." Chute's voice was firm.

Maybe if she hadn't said anything, I would've tried to slip between the pillar beams. But what was I going to do once I was in there? I had no weapon, no training. I couldn't even slice time yet. I was just going to get in the way. So I stood there looking at the endless parade of crawlers flow from the fire and the Paladins tireless efforts to control them. But they were starting to tire. They weren't blinking into timeslices anymore. They were conserving their energy, fighting them in real time.

"I'm not going to lose you again." Chute stepped next to me. Her cheeks were glowing in the yellow aura. "I don't care who you think you are or what you can do, you'll die if you go in there."

Panic was clenching my chest. What could I do then? What? If the duplicates got through the portal, what was next? Something in Rudder's knowledge told me the Paladins didn't have a backup plan. They had gambled on their move to end the existence of the duplicates and now the whole world was on the table. Winner takes all.

"We can get to Buxbee's lab." Streeter felt lucid. The slack in his face had taken up.

"What do I need to do?" I asked.

"The security shells need to be completed."

"How do I do that?"

He looked at me. "You want me to tell you now?"

"Just… just think it." I closed my eyes, focused on his mind. I could absorb what he knew the instant it came up, but it was a murky cloud of thoughts.

"What the hell are you talking about?" Streeter said.

"I got to know how to finish that security shell or those things could get into virtualmode." I stepped toward him. "They're dupes, Streeter."

Like that was all I needed to say, he would figure out the rest. But he was staring at me like there was a tiny dragon attached to my neck.

"I've got to finish the security updates," I said.

"No, you're not," Chute said. "You see what's going on back there? You're not going anywhere near that school. Neither of you."

"Buxbee's gear is only coded for me," Streeter said. "It'll reject you. You can't get on."

That was a problem, but I'd figure it out later. If Rudder would get the clamp completely deactivated, I could slice time and have plenty of time. *Come on, Rudder. Faster.* I felt him twitch, impatiently.

"Look, there's no danger if I go," Streeter said. "Buxbee's lab is all the way on the other side of the school. Those yellow beams got that truck barricaded around the Pit. Whatever's on the inside isn't getting out. We can go log in and get it done, in and out. If you're helping, I can finish in like five or ten minutes."

"I'm going," Chute said.

"No, you're not," I snapped.

"Yes. I am."

"Look." I gently gripped her bicep. "This is—"

She yanked her arm out. "I'm going with you. Try to stop me."

"I will."

Sometimes she hit me in the arm when I acted like an asshole. Sometimes she just set her feet. Always, she got her way because she usually made more sense than me, thought clearer. This time, I was right. But this time, she didn't swing and didn't dig in to get her way. I felt her energy soften.

"Don't make me stay out here," she said. "I can't just wait."

"It's too dangerous."

"I can help."

"I wouldn't forgive myself if something happened to you."

"Neither would I."

I took a breath and looked around. Truth be told, I didn't want to leave her. I didn't want to be away from her, not when this was going on. Maybe it was selfish to let her

177

come along, but was she any safer out here? I would never know the answer to that.

We started for Buxbee's lab.

WALKING ON SHELLS

Lights were on a portion of the hall, but beyond that it faded to black. Dust drizzled down like mist. Buxbee's door was partly open. The classroom was so dark the desks and chairs looked like lumps waiting to jump us.

"What now?" I said.

"We virtualmode," Streeter said. "It's the only way to finish the upgrade."

"I thought virtualmode was shut down."

"Yeah, unless you've got high-security access. That would be me."

"You can't just call it up on a monitor?"

"Maybe." He sounded thoughtful. "But I'm not sure."

"Can you do it or not?"

I could see him turn to me but couldn't see his expression. It felt hot.

"Look, we can't afford to leave the skin," I said. "I don't care if those things are trapped out there or not, we need to call it up on a monitor."

"Well, now's a perfect time to experiment, wouldn't you say?" he snapped. "I'll boot up the monitors and break out the manual so we can work in the skin. Got a light?"

I didn't like it, either. Streeter was staring at me, waiting for an answer. *Which is it?* Somehow, I had become the leader and he was waiting for my blessing. I just couldn't bring myself to say it. They shouldn't be here. They should be at home or out there with the cops and EMTs. This was a bad idea to bring them along, but I had to get honest, I couldn't do it alone.

Chute's touch broke the tension. Her fingers slid down my arm and laced with mine. "How long will it take if we virtualmode?" she asked.

"Five minutes," Streeter said. "Maybe ten."

"What'd you mean 'we'?" I said. "You're not going."

"I'll stay and watch things, make sure it's all right. You and Streeter go, get it done. We're wasting time."

Her smile was forced. Streeter said, "Then make that twenty minutes if she's not coming."

"Why?" I asked.

"Look, you want to sit here and debate every possible scenario? Jesus Christ, we'd be done if we jumped on as soon as we got here."

"All right! Let's get on." I dropped into a soft seat. "But you're staying, Chute."

She gave me that same smile.

Streeter grumbled as he sat down and stuck the transporters behind his ears. As soon as I applied them, I was in my sim. The gray space around us went on forever. Streeter's giant sim stood next to a hovering bluish ball.

"This is a replica of the portal," he said. "There are shells around it that monitor access. The only way to virtualmode is through it. Anyone, or any*thing,* that tries to access it illegally will not get through. If those things reach the portal below the Pit, they'll have to come through this in order to virtualmode onto the worldwide Internet. If they don't get through this, then they're just stuck in a hole with nowhere to go."

A black figure flickered between us, and then Chute was standing there. She pushed the dark cowl from her head. "Hey."

I just shook my head. She knew how to play me. Now it was either argue with her about getting off while the clock ran or shut up. "Let's just get this over with," I said.

The portal was enclosed in several translucent shells, the last one partially complete. "We need to finish the final shell to make the portal impenetrable," he said. "Then we get off. Done."

Streeter reached into the empty space beside him, his hairy fingers grasping something invisible. He took several breaths, closed his eyes and muttered something as though he were wishing for something. Then, between his dirty fingernails, a curved puzzle piece appeared. He hunched over and slid it into a gap in the unfinished shell.

"Anything we can do?" Chute said.

Streeter twitched. The piece dissolved. He let out a deep breath and bowed his head. "Yeah, how about not scaring the shit out of me?"

"Do you really need the giant sim with the fat fingers?" she said. "There's no one here to fight, you know."

"Oh, sure. Give me an hour and I'll build another sim."

"Don't give me that, you've got generic sims in reserve. I've seen them."

"You don't know what I—"

"Can we get on with this?" I said.

Streeter blew a curly lock of hair from his eyes and stared at Chute. "I have to recall the pieces and fit them into the shell. You can hold each one in place for about ten seconds or until the piece stitches while I retrieve the others."

He held up his hand and, again, a piece appeared between his fingers five seconds later. He bent over, carefully placing it. Chute put her finger on it and he created another piece, put it in place and I held it. He did it again. Now Chute held two of them. I let go of my piece to grab the next and it disappeared.

"Longer, Socket," Streeter said. "You got to give the stitching code time to lock it in place."

"You said ten seconds."

"I said *about* ten seconds," he said, bringing another piece to where the first one just evaporated.

I kept my finger on this one as long as I could. Streeter pulled them down faster, sliding each one in place and barking at us to hold them tighter and longer. We had no more fingers left. Streeter paused to give the pieces extra time to stitch. When they were a shade darker, we let go and he started after more.

"Halfway there," he said.

We took deep breaths and began again. It was getting stuffy. Buxbee's lab must've been overheating. Streeter had most of our fingers occupied when the gray space trembled and two pieces crumbled from the shell.

"They're coming," Streeter said.

"What do you mean *they're coming?*" I said.

Streeter moved faster, with both hands, and brought two pieces down. "As soon as those things make contact with the portal, they could come through this ball right here." He clicked the pieces in place. "We have to have this final shell done to keep them inside."

Distant thunder shook somewhere. "Why does it sound like they're out there?" I said.

"Focus, Socket!"

Streeter hauled the pieces out faster then we could hold them. Chute used her chin on one of them. Three crumbled.

Streeter had to stop adding pieces and help hold them until they stitched.

"What'll they do if they get here?" Chute said.

He took the time to put two more pieces in place before answering. "Well, seeing as this isn't finished, they'll shatter the security shells, blow by us and roam free in virtualmode." He flicked his eyes at me. "You'll have to ask Mr. Secret Agent what they'll do after that."

I pretended not to notice, like we needed to be focusing and not talking. But I didn't know what they were going to do if they got free. I had one of those feelings there was a lot riding on getting this shell completed because the Paladins were out there fighting like it was life or death.

"Will they come after us?" Chute asked.

When I didn't answer, Streeter said, "Probably not."

"Probably? What's that mean?"

"I don't know, it means probably. Maybe those things don't care about us, they just want inside. Or..." He took a second to place a piece. "Or maybe they'll be pissed off that we were trying to stop them and... you know."

"You know?" Chute's fingers wiggled enough to shatter two pieces. Streeter started to say something, but Chute cut him off. "No, I don't know!"

Streeter took a deep breath and went back to concentrating. He should've been doing what I was doing, but now it was too late. The side of his head was getting a full-bore stare from Chute.

"Chute," I said. "Maybe you should get off, we're almost done."

She turned the heat on me. "No. And don't ask me that again."

Another disturbance rattled close by. We held the pieces tighter.

"Hurry," Chute whispered.

"*As fast as I can,*" Streeter sang, grabbing two more pieces.

"Why weren't you grabbing two pieces to begin with?" she said.

"This isn't easy!" He shoved them in place. "I got to concentrate."

"But they're coming," she urged.

"I KNOW THAT!" He stopped for a second to refocus, then retrieved two more pieces.

The next disturbance vibrated through my sim. I felt that one. Maybe it was because the clamp was shutting down and I was getting back to normal, but the timeslice spark still wasn't ready. Rudder wasn't done. The look on Streeter and Chute's faces meant they felt it, too.

"Ten more," Streeter said, huffing.

"You can do it," I said.

Two more pieces locked in. The shell darkened. We had our fingers splayed out over as many pieces as we could hold.

Kaaaaboooooom!

The portal shuddered under our hands. We lost a piece.

"Three more!" Streeter shouted. "Hold them!"

The gray space transformed, swirling like fog, dense and grainy. Footsteps echoed under the distant thunder. Someone was out there, shoes clicking on a hard floor. I looked around, listening. There it was again! Footsteps echoed, closer this time. Was Streeter wrong? Were they coming in from somewhere else? Did they already get through another portal somewhere in the world and now they were coming to open this one?

"WILL YOU CONCENTRATE?" Streeter shouted. "Only two more, just focus on these next two, all right?"

"Chute, get off, now," I said. "I can hold the rest. Get off."

"You can't hold all the pieces. He'll be done in a second and we can all get off."

Streeter pulled the final piece down, held it delicately over the last hole. Our fingers filled the gap, holding the last pieces in place. He waited with the last one, his chest heaving.

"All right," he said, quietly, "let them go."

We took our fingers out, holding our breath. The pieces trembled, but held. The shell went two shades darker. Streeter so carefully laid the last one over the gap and touched it with the tip of his finger, pushed it into place. The shell clicked and turned black.

"There." He exhaled so long his shoulders deflated. "The portal is locked."

KAAABOOOOOOM!

The floor tilted.

Chute dropped to her knees; Streeter teetered forward on the tips of his toes, windmilling his arms to keep his balance. I couldn't stop the virtual giant from falling on top of the portal. He didn't just graze it: he pushed it all the way to the floor, bounced on it and flopped on his back. The portal bounced back to its original position. It bobbed between us. We stood extra still, not even breathing, while the portal jiggled in place.

A hairline fracture slithered across the black shell. Piece by piece, it crumbled until every single shell lay at Streeter's feet. The portal glittered blue and white, bright as ever.

A mechanical screech called from inside the portal, like a crystal ball playing the near future.

EeeeeeeeeeeeeieiiiiiIIIIIIIIIII!

"They're in," Streeter said.

"What now?" I said.

"You've got powers, right?" Streeter said. "Fight them."

"FIGHT THEM?"

"Aren't you stronger, or something?"

"Do you see a cape on my back?"

"Those guys up there in the parking lot, they were disappearing and reappearing and slinging some badass weapons. You telling me you can't do that?"

"I'm not like that." *I don't know what I am.*

"Streeter," Chute said, "can we hide the portal somewhere else?"

Streeter's mouth contorted, about to shout his frustration, then stopped. "That just might…" He placed both hands over the portal, his lips moving, eyes closed. His muttering grew louder, like an enchantment and a clear shell wrapped around the portal, snapping shut.

"That's a basic security shell," he said. "But it will buy us some time. I can set up transportation coordinates to an obscure website and take the portal with us. It'll confuse them. They'll find us, eventually, but it'll give us a few minutes."

"How much time do we have?" I said.

He shrugged. "It's hard to say."

"Guess."

"They'll be looking for us in ten minutes, maybe twelve."

"Well, do it," I said.

He took the portal in his hands and closed his eyes, whispering new coordinates. The echoing footsteps started again. I circled Streeter, searching for the source. They grew louder.

"Hurry, Streeter."

He muttered louder, not hearing me. Hands clenched in concentration, his fingertips denting the shell. Someone whispered my name. *Socket.* I jumped next to Streeter, hands up, knees bent. Chute beside me.

A white, generic sim appeared out of the fog, its hands folded behind its back. It had no eyes, ears or nose. A slit opened, where a mouth would've been, imitating a smile.

It said, "Salutations."

FALSE PROPHET

"Broak?"

"Indeed, it is." His voice was distorted, hardly recognizable.

"How'd he get here?" Streeter hid the portal, deftly concealing it behind his back.

"My dear ogre friend, I'm sure you're well aware of what would happen if the duplicates' crawlers get through this portal. We want to be sure no one, or *thing*, has tampered with the security shells." He kicked at shattered pieces and they rang on the end of his foot. "It appears I'm a tad late."

"They put you in charge?" I said.

"They are a bit busy, as I'm sure you have noticed. The entire world is under attack, my dear Socket. The duplicates have launched a full-scale attack and I'm afraid we were caught, as you might say, with our trousers down."

His face twitched where eyebrows would normally be. "We are using every last resource to stave them off. It is the last stand, my friend. It just so happens I have come to help you protect this compromised portal security shell." He looked down at the pieces again and held out his hand. "If you would've completed your assignment, you wouldn't be in this mess, dear ogre. You have failed. I suggest you turn the security over to one more suitable."

"I don't think so," Streeter said.

Broak tilted his head toward me. "Can you talk some sense into your friend? The world is at stake, you know."

"You tried to kill me, you piece of shit." I rammed my hand around his neck, wedged my finger and thumb under his jawbone. He did not resist. "I'd be dead if it wasn't for Pivot."

"Can we put that aside for now, dear Socket? There are greater issues before us than a street fight."

I threw him so far into the gray fog he almost disappeared. I wanted to break him in half, somehow reach through that sim and choke him, make his throat burn like mine did. Maybe I couldn't beat his ass in a straight up fight, at least not until I got control of time again.

"I can explain my actions." Broak righted himself and folded his arms behind his back as he walked back. "It is difficult to understand my motivation, but if you give me a moment I will do so. However, do be reasonable, dear Socket. We do not have a moment to spare. If you grant me the portal, there will soon be time to explain everything. I beg of you."

Mechanical screeching called from inside the portal.

"I am capable of a 200-cube security shell within five minutes," he said. "I have the programming loaded in this sim and can secure it before it's too late."

He took a step closer. Gray fog whooshed around our ankles, muffling his footsteps.

"We have the technology. You have seen it yourself. Do the right thing and put our conflict aside. Can you do that?"

The slit-mouth did not smile. The generic face had no expression. The world couldn't afford for us to fail. They needed us. They needed the Paladins. They needed *him*. I had to admit it: Broak was more qualified than me. And that way, Chute and Streeter could get back to their skin.

"There's no time to debate this, I want the portal." Broak took another step and our sims shifted into battle garb. Weapons unfolded on my hip. A battle stave materialized in Chute's hand.

"What're you doing, Streeter?" Chute said. "We don't need this stuff."

He looked at the nicked battleaxe dangling from the barbarian belt criss-crossing his chest, the studded war boots and spiked battle gloves. "The battle alert just triggered. There's a threat nearby."

"I'm not going to ask again." The slit-smile creased Broak's face.

"Streeter!" Chute cried.

Broak unfolded his arms from behind his back. His fingers fused together like spears. He lunged like a swordsman, his arm plunging through Streeter's stomach, the axe clattering away. Broak's arm-sword slid all the way through Streeter, wrapping around the portal. In the next instant, he yanked it halfway through Streeter's body.

"Cut it!" Streeter grabbed Broak's arm with both hands. "Cut his arm off!"

I grabbed the evolver clubs from my belt. They unfolded and fused around my hands and forearms and I tried to focus on a weapon. So many of them jumbled in my head; I couldn't concentrate. It happened too fast. I couldn't take my eyes off the gaping wound in Streeter's stomach spewing molten gray goo. Chute jabbed her battle stave at Broak's face, but he caught it with his free hand.

"Don't make this mistake," Broak hissed. "The world needs me to have this!"

He yanked again and pulled Streeter toward him, but the virtual mass of the giant sim could not be taken down. Streeter resisted and they played tug-of-war, the portal half buried in Streeter's spleen.

"CUT THE GODDAMN ARM OFF!" Streeter yelled.

I shook my head, closed my eyes and held my breath. An image formed and twin curved sabers emerged from my hands. Broak kicked my knee, breaking it backwards. Bones cracked and I went flying, but the tip of a saber caught his arm, severing it from Streeter. Broak tumbled, ripping the battle stave from Chute's grip. His slit turned upside down. His arms flattened into edged blades.

"I will clear the chaff," he cried, getting to his feet and criss-crossing his executioner's arms above his head, "before reaping the harvest!"

He was too powerful. Too skilled. I managed to stand on one leg, but it was all I could do. He would cut me in half, send me back to the skin. The gleaming arms rose higher. I envisioned an evolver shield, but there was Chute. I would not leave her, even if it meant leaving the portal in his charge.

A fat hand gripped my arm.

The fog thickened, turned gray to black.

I left.

To the in-between.

Walls built from out of the dark and surrounded us in a wood-paneled room. Stuffed heads of antelope and grizzly bear formed on the walls. A fireplace blazed. Broak was gone.

"What happened?" Chute pushed the cowl off her face.

Streeter lay sprawled on the floor, his head wedged against the couch. The glowing portal peeked from a gap in his stomach, and lit up his chest. Broak's limp, white arm lay across him, fingers stuck in the portal's shell.

"I got news for you," Streeter said. "Broak sucks ass." I grabbed his arm and tried to pull him to his feet. "Don't bother. He destroyed my spine. I don't have time to rebuild it." He pulled the portal out of his sucking guts, pushing back his intestines. He plucked Broak's hand from the portal shell and tossed it against the wall where it smacked like a piece of wet liver. He handed the portal to me. "You're going to have to take it."

Several more pieces of the basic shell fell away, exposing the bare portal beneath.

"Make sure you don't touch the portal directly," Streeter said. "Buxbee always warned if the shells failed to never, ever touch it. He didn't say why, he just warned us. But he also said the shells would never fail, so maybe he doesn't know what he's talking about."

Chute looked out the cabin's frosty window. "Is this the Rime?"

"It was the first place I could find in my virtualmode history. I didn't have a lot of time to evaluate locations. There was an arm in me at the time."

"But the Rime?" Chute turned on him. "They're going to know we're in here and then what?"

"Hey, let me stick my fist through you and see how clearly you think."

"You've been back here, haven't you? You've been hacking back into—" Chute ducked just as one of Streeter's battle hatchets helicoptered over her head. It buried in the wall. I stopped her before she staked his head into the floor. She walked off counting out loud.

"That guy wasn't planning on protecting the portal, Socket," Streeter said. "I don't care what you say."

I didn't know what Broak was doing. He was the Paladins' darling, so maybe he had orders to protect it at all costs. After all, it wasn't like he was trying to kill *us*, just

191

our sims. But Streeter was right, there was something off, no need for superpowers to see that. The guy was a head case, but he was up to something. I cradled the portal carefully, holding it up to my ear. The screeches echoed far away.

"It might take them five minutes or so to figure out the portal is in the Rime," Streeter said. "Virtually, this is a large world and that means it contains a lot of data. They'll have to sort through it all to locate the portal, especially if you hide it somewhere. Find a waterfall—something with massive dataflow."

"What're you going to do?" I asked.

"Stay here, what else? You couldn't carry me with a tank."

"I don't like leaving you." Chute was across the room, arms folded and fingers tapping. Poking him with her stave was one thing, but leaving him with those things was another.

"It's just a sim," Streeter said. "I'll build a new one."

"Yeah, but you said they might be able to hurt us."

He smashed his elbow through the wood floor, sending splinters up to the ceiling. "I'll hide under the cabin, if that makes you feel better."

I dropped to my working knee, and helped him pull up the floor. "You sure about this?"

"We don't have a choice. You got to keep that portal safe as long as you can. Whatever you do, don't let Whitey get it." Streeter rolled from the floor onto the frozen ground beneath. "Head west, along the ridge. There's a network of caves at the foot of the hills. Don't ask how I know. Get lost and maybe they'll never locate the portal."

The floorboards rebuilt themselves, dirty and scuffed, as though they'd been there the whole time. "GO!" Streeter's muffled voice shouted through the floor.

Chute watched me limp onto the porch. She took the portal from me and tucked it into a bag. We stopped at the edge of the weathered steps and looked up at the gray sky and blowing snow. *Seems like just yesterday.*

"Maybe one of us should get back to the skin," I said. "Maybe—"

"Forget it," Chute said. "I'm not leaving."

I clenched my fist, hoping I could timeslice, but the spark wasn't bright enough. Face it, I was more like her than I was a Paladin. She tossed her lookits and they zipped into the trees. She loped down the hill like a deer, hit the trickling stream at the bottom and started up the other side, the pregnant sack bouncing off her leg. I followed, half-stepping with my left leg, the knee still not working. She slowed down just so I could catch up.

The trees all looked the same and soon the path ended. We slowly picked our way through the forest until we reached the next ridge. We stopped on a stone outcropping that overlooked ten thousand acres of white treetops. Walnut-sized snowflakes blotted out the sun.

Streeter was right, the Rime was huge. With all the dataflow needed to keep it running, we would be like grains of sand on a long beach. A lookit spy returned from the trees and warbled in her ear.

"There's a small cave a quarter-mile down this side."

The hill was steep. I couldn't slow down, not with the gimpy leg, and ended up rolling half the way. I bounced off trees and tumbled from rocky ledges. Chute hooked an arm around my waist, hauling me to level ground. We splashed through a stream. My leg was hardly working by then.

The water weaved between snow-covered boulders and fell over a cliff. We stopped at the edge of the waterfall, the water dropping twenty feet into a pool of rising steam.

"It's over there," she said. The opening to the cave was partially obscured by heavy spruce branches. "Let's follow it into the mountain. Streeter said the more we get lost, the harder it will be to find us."

We leaped together, arm-in-arm, torpedoing down the waterfall to the bottom of the pool. Our battle gear was too heavy for swimming, so we climbed out. Chute wrung out her cape, throwing it over her shoulder. We were well protected by ancient conifers and cliffs. The wind howled high above, but at the mouth of the cave it was as still as dawn.

"Come on." Chute moved ahead, dotting the virgin snow. "Let's get inside before we freeze solid."

Ice crystals formed on my nose. My pants crunched. Chute held the branches out of the way and I hobbled into the dreary darkness. The portal glowed through Chute's pouch, silent ever since we left the cabin.

"Got a light?" I said.

"Hold on." She felt around. "It's in here somewhere."

Just pull out the portal. Or forget it; we'll walk in the dark. I never said either of those things. A snaky sensation rolled in my guts and seized my mind. Something was in there—with us.

"Will this do?" A dim light flickered in someone's palm, glowing brighter, illuminating his white face and body. "Dear Socket?"

MONSTER AND MONSTERS

We ran from the cave but I fell headfirst into the snow. Chute stooped to help me to my feet. "Go!" I yanked away. "Take the portal and go!"

Chute pulled me through the snow. Behind us, Broak watched with his hands on his hips, both arms intact. Slit-mouth turned up.

"What'd you want?" she shouted. "You want this?" She tore away the pouch. "You want to save the world by yourself, is that what you came for? Well, here, go save the world, hero!"

"No!" I caught the corner of the pouch and it landed at my feet. "Don't give it to him."

"He's going to shred our sims, so what?" She squatted down, put her arms around my chest and sat me up.

"I'm going to be saving the world, indeed," he said, "though perhaps not as you envision."

195

Broak eased the portal out of the pouch. His generic face radiated pale blue. He turned it around, admired the swirling colors. He snapped off a piece of the shell and sank his fingers into the portal. It jiggled like a gooey mass and jumped away, at first, then oozed up his wrist. The opaque whiteness of his skin darkened. Blue flames ignited from inside the portal, creeping up his arm. Veins pulsed up his shoulder, bulging like slithering purple snakes. The flames wrapped around his shoulders then engulfed his entire body, the whiteness giving way to fleshy color. The details of his skin-body took form and absorbed the flames and then he was there, the real Broak. Black eyes, black hair and perfect teeth.

He stretched, admiring his hand, front and back. Smiled. "Welcome to a new era, dear friends."

"What just happened?" Chute's voice quivered.

The portal was the same colors as the wormhole Mom drove through. The same as the sacred portal deep below the Garrison that ripped me from my skin, took me somewhere through space and time. The portal was a transporter, too; transporting our awareness from skin to sim. But he was, in a sense, making direct contact with it. Did it transport *him?* Was that really Broak? Did he bring his skin into virtualmode?

He twirled around, head back and arms extended catching snowflakes on his tongue. Snow crunched under his feet as he giggled. He didn't want to save the portal, he wanted to use it. Broak had nothing to do with the Paladins. And if he wasn't a Paladin...

"You're a duplicate."

He bent down next to me. "That is very astute, dear Socket, but incorrect. I am not a duplicate, but it is true I am no longer associated with the Paladin Nation. They will find my skin in the Garrison connected to a portal, but it is of no use to me now. That heart need beat no longer."

"You never had a heart. You're a traitor."

"Of course I had a heart. I am flesh and blood, but never was my heart with the Paladins. I find them to be soiled and imperfect." He tilted his head, looking for the right word. "Too *human*."

"They created you. How could you betray them?"

"They *created* me." He chuckled. "Do you hear yourself? They *created me*. Does that sound human to you?" His lip quivered. "They *built* me, *manufactured* me, put breath in my lungs and told me what to do. Does that sound human to you? Mmmm?" He nudged me with his boot. "Mmmm, tell me, does it?"

Chute slid back, pulled me with her. Broak planted the tip of his boot into my shattered knee. My leg flopped like a rag, crackling like a bag of rocks.

"DOES THAT SOUND HUMAN TO YOU?" he bellowed.

His smooth cheeks flushed with rage, he went to the cave and stared into the darkness, collecting his thoughts. He was feeling something, needed to get it under control.

When he turned back to us, his smile was a perfect mask. "The duplicates showed me the way. If life is good, why waste it with imperfection? Duplicates make decisions based on fact, not feelings. You will see, dear Socket. The world will be a better place when the duplications make decisions. There will be no more corruption, only perfection."

"They're imitations. Not real."

"Who says they're not real? They think, they laugh, they feel. I believe those are the characteristics that define you and me as human, isn't that so? Mmmm?"

"Who said we're supposed to be perfect?"

He tilted his head, looking all too much like Spindle. "Who says we shouldn't?"

Screeches called from the portal. Broak held it to his ear, swayed back and forth. His eyes fluttered and closed. "Let's get on with the task at hand, shall we?"

He yanked me toward him with effortless strength—so quickly that Chute fell over my shoulder. She boxed him in the middle of the face, pulling me away with her other arm. Broak grabbed my hand. He casually wiped the blood trickling out his nose and looked disgusted.

"They wanted to kill you, dear Socket. The duplicates wanted their crawlers to unlock the virtualmode and kill you at the same time." He shook his head, tsking. "Those darn imitations are so efficient. Always multi-tasking."

"Why do they want virtualmode?"

"Why, to get back to the source, of course. They share the same desire as humans, you see. They crave to be connected with the source of their creation just as humans seek peace in their so-called soul. They were born of the virtualmode universe, they cannot survive without it. Paladins sought to cut them off from their life source, but they did not foresee the size of the snake they were taunting. The duplicates cannot be stopped. There are just too many of them. Too bad they didn't have that dirty rat Pivot to tell the Paladins this truth." He leaned in and whispered, "The world is ours, now."

I struck with my rigid fingers, aiming to split his face in half. He caught my wrist and broke it, my fingers went limp, and then in one smooth motion he plunged my hand into the portal. Blue flames crept up my arm to my shoulder. My teeth tingled. I struggled, but Broak held me firm. Chute swatted at the flames walking around my neck, encircling my chest. Veins swelled on the back of my hand. White hair fell over my face.

My sim doesn't have white hair.

The flames stalled and flickered, then rushed around me and Chute like we were bales of dry straw. My hand burned. My smashed knee ached.

Cold nipped at my cheeks.

Frozen fabric pressed against my skin.

Chute screamed.

The pain came all at once. Shattered bones and broken nerves radiated like nails into my knee. Chute squeezed tighter.

"Baaill... bail..." My lips were stiff and numb. "Code... bailll out code bail."

"Welcome, dear friends, to your new skin!" Broak raised his arms. "Sometimes you feel pleasure, sometimes you feel... *pain.*"

I blacked out.

Chute was rocking me back and forth when I came to. "What's going on, Socket?"

Her teeth chattered. That's when I noticed her hands wrapped over my chest. They were fleshy. She was shaking.

"I did not bring you here to murder, dear Socket." Broak paced restlessly toward the cave. "I will admit I tried to end your life in the Graveyard, yes. Forgive me for that, will you, dear friend? Because since then, I have had an epiphany. I cannot take credit for this brilliant idea. It was my mentor that understood your true potential. This was all his idea, yes."

The portal swelled to twice its size in his hands. It was screeching.

"If you will excuse me a moment."

He dug his fingers in and pulled it open. The remains of the shell twinkled onto his feet. He smiled, at first, then grunted. His arms bulged as the portal attempted to close, forcing Broak to one knee for leverage. He stretched it open again and this time a jointed stick poked through, feeling around. Another poked out and then another until there were eight. The jointed sticks helped hold the portal open until it gave birth to a putty-colored glob.

The crawler fell into the snow, then rose up like a newborn calf, its body pulsing. Two more plopped next to it, all three shaking on new legs, growing with each pulsation.

"I will admit, your death seemed to be the only solution." Broak tossed the portal aside. "The duplicates already find Paladins a formidable opponent; they couldn't have you making the Nation stronger, faster and smarter. They wanted you dead. But then my mentor came up with an idea, not just a way to eliminate you but a way to steal you from them."

The crawlers were already double their original size, spiking their legs into the ground. Broak stroked their backs.

"You see, my friends are going to pull you apart and integrate your genetic code into our database. Your DNA will be the blueprint for new and improved duplications. You will help us, dear Socket. You will become one of us." He smiled wide and whispered. "Is that not wonderful?"

SAVIOR

Chute tried to lift me, but I screamed at the effort. She slid me to the water, panting. Her foot plunked into the pool. The crawlers' bodies beat like hearts, watching us struggle with their brightening eyelights. Broak edged closer.

"Don't fret, dear Socket." He wiped the water from my cheek. "You're going on to a better life."

Chute slapped his hand. "Don't touch him!"

He only smiled and went back to his pets, now shoulder tall, bobbing and weaving. He rubbed their bodies. They nuzzled back.

"As you can see, we have everything the Paladins have. Technology is our specialty."

"You're not a duplicate," I said.

"Not yet." He held out his arms. "But soon, I will download into a fabricated body of my choice. I will determine my fate. I will be the captain of my life." His energy darkened, casting a shadow over his face. "Do you think I want to be victimized by those Paladins any longer? Slave to the human race, mmm? I am my own god now, dear Socket. I can become whatever I want in the real world. What's not real about that, mmm? Why would humans resist their heart's desire? They are far too selfish not to follow. And here's the big surprise, my dear one. Are you ready for it?" He stood straight and his expression brightened. "You're coming with me."

Chute whimpered, pulling me deeper into the water. I was struggling just to keep from screaming. "There's... nothing real... about you."

"Well, if I'm no longer real..." He kicked my broken knee. The pain radiated like electricity. "Maybe that will change your mind."

I could hold the scream in no longer.

"Rejoice!" Broak shouted with his back to us, his voice echoing into the cave. "Mankind will no longer toil in incompetence."

My teeth clattered. Chute's breath was warm on my ear.

"Humanity's suffering will come to an end! We will put the world in order. The human race will evolve into a super species of choice and freedom!"

The timeslicing spark flashed inside me. Brighter. Firmer. I wrapped my mind around it and colors swirled. Snowflakes staggered. Broak lifted his arms, palms to the sky, surrounded by a halo of light.

I sliced time.

Energy filled me, pouring into every muscle and every broken bone. In the dead silence, I closed my eyes and searched out the source of my agony. I traveled through my own veins, penetrating tissues and nerves. I knew the ways of my body intimately, and commanded it to heal. Cartilage reconnected in my knees, bones fused together in my wrist. Pain was arrested.

But the spark slipped like a greased rat, squirming from my grip. Nerve lines screamed again. A crawler lifted Broak onto its back. Broak squeezed it between his knees, his face lifted to the heavens.

"Do that again," Chute said. "Whatever you just did, do it again. You felt stronger."

"I... can't." The spark was dim. It was too soon. "I'm sorry I got you into this."

"Don't say sorry." She squeezed tighter. "Don't you say that!"

"Flawless." Broak almost sang the word, the hard line of his brow darkening his eyes. "That is what we'll bring them, dear Socket. Unadulterated perfection."

His choppy laughter echoed over the trees. I chased the spark again, squeezed it every direction I could, but it avoided me. *Rudder! Please, bring it back.*

The crawlers reared up on their hind legs like wild stallions and unleashed a screech, blowing the hair away from my face. Blood rushed past my throbbing eardrums. Chute scrambled deeper, dragging me with her. Water crept above my waist.

"We are saviors." He raised the portal with both hands. "Rejoice... for it is at hand, dear Socket... rejoice for I WILL LEAD THEM TO THE PROMISELAND!!"

The crawlers reared again, their jointed legs aimed at us. They would pull me apart, study every cell and every strand of DNA. They would become stronger because of me. They would become faster because of me. People would suffer. The world, the real world, would end. It would end because of me. I didn't want this. Pivot was wrong. I was no hero, I was a curse. The world would pay, because of me.

"*LOOK OUT!*" Streeter's voice vibrated in my skull. *CccrrraaaaaAAAACCCKKKKKKKKK!*

203

A flash, then blindness. Deafness. The percussion stopped my heart and the world spun.

Colder. And wetter.

Frigidness stole the feeling from my skin and the air from my lungs. I opened my mouth and sucked a mouthful of water. My wet clothes pulled me down. I couldn't tell which way was up until I hit the rocky bottom. I tried to kick upward, but my leg would not work. I heaved myself up, but the surface was too far away. I wouldn't get there. My lungs blazed and unconsciousness settled around me like a warm blanket. My hand slipped and I fell. I scrambled again, but felt myself drifting.

Something grabbed my wrist and yanked me up. Once. Twice. Three times, someone pulled at me with frantic desperation. Darkness had settled on my wide-open eyes.

Something soft and warm pressed on my lips, blew air into my chest. It happened again. And then I puked warm water.

"Oh, god," I blubbered, rolling over.

"Socket." Chute grabbed my tunic and shook me. "Oh, thank God you're all right! I thought you were gone."

The world was bleached and bleary. Water dripped off Chute's chattering chin. Her eyes were red and misty. Her hair smelled sulfuric. We lay on muddy ground; the snow was gone.

"What happened?" I asked.

She sat back on her knees. "Lightning."

I turned my head. A blackened crater sizzled at the mouth of the cave, smoke rising from the center. The crawlers' misshapen bodies were scattered around, their legs twisted and bent.

Chute helped me stand, our water-soaked clothes already stiffening in the arctic air, but it kept me numb. I hobbled with her help to the smoking crater. Broak lay in the bottom. The left half of his chest was missing, as was his left arm. His hair and clothes had evaporated to his waist, revealing skin blistered like tar. Perfect teeth gleamed through holes in his cheeks. The portal, blue and glittering, lay wedged under his arm.

"Holy shit." Streeter's voice echoed in my skull. *"I just fried those assholes like butter. I'm sorry it took so long, I don't have the control panels in this crawl space and I wanted to build a lightning bolt with enough voltage to melt them like plastic."* He chuckled. *"They won't virtualmode for months. Not in those sims."*

Chute couldn't look away. She began to shake, pushing me away and staring at the bottom of the crater. She tried to speak. I held her close but she pushed again. "This isn't happening... this isn't..."

I turned her from the scene, held her closer. Tensed and shaking, she tried to fight me off. I held her until she went limp. She laid her head on my shoulder and wept. We stayed that way, swaying back and forth while she cried.

"Socket?" Streeter said. *"Chute? Can you hear me?"*

I told Streeter what happened. I told him about the awareness transference, and how our sims had become skin. We couldn't log off. We could smell things. We could *feel.*

"Impossible."

"The portal, Streeter... there's something about the portal being a transporter. When I touched it, our sims became skin. We're here, Streeter. We're not back in the lab, we're actually here."

He babbled on, argued and shouted. "I told you not to touch—"

"Listen!" I cut him off. "None of that's important. It's done! Now, how do we get out of here? There has to be a way to get back to our skin."

"The portal. If you destroy the portal it'll send you back. It pulled you out of your skin, you should return if it's destroyed."

"Can you redress us?" Chute let go, her teeth clicking together. "We need dry clothes, Streeter. Warm, dry ones."

"Yeah, yeah... I can do that."

The hard frozen clothes faded, simultaneously replaced with identical garb and a hot, soft coat. Cold still penetrated my bones. I went back to the crater. The portal was there. Steam hissed from cracks along Broak's blackened body.

"I didn't mean to kill him, Socket," Streeter said, softly. *"I thought... I didn't know he was real."*

"I know."

"Maybe he's not dead. Maybe he bolted back to his skin and I fried his sim. That's all I was trying to do, you know."

But Broak didn't return to his skin. He was at the bottom of a burned-out hole. The look on his face said he hadn't even seen it coming. I doubt he felt a thing.

"I'm sorry," Streeter said. *"I didn't mean to do it. I didn't kill him, did I? I'm not—"*

"He probably escaped, Streeter," I lied. "Now tell me, how do I destroy that thing?"

There was a long pause. *"Use your evolver,"* he said, uneasily. *"Just cut the thing in half."*

Chute stood next to me, wrinkling her nose. The unmistakable smell of fried skin wafted up from the pit, clinging to the back of my throat. I breathed through my mouth without pinching my nose and sat on the crater's edge. I slid down the side a few feet and avoided touching the body. I fumbled for the portal, coaxing it with my fingertips. It was stuck. I slid closer, hooked my hand around it. It broke away with a wet snap. Chute stepped into the crater and held out her hand. Something yanked me back.

"Socket!" Chute screamed.

Broak had my arm. Bones protruded from his crispy fingertips. His head turned and crackled, and flakes of blackened skin fell away. His eye sockets were empty, and his tongue darted out, licking what remained of his lips. He pulled me closer.

"Dear Socket..."

His hand trembled. The tongue fell back into his mouth. No. Broak did not make it back to the skin.

BURIED

We lay the portal on the ground. I pulled the evolver from my waist and let it unfold around my arm, piercing my nerve lines. Never before had I felt an evolver tap into my nervous system. I imagined a weapon: A long, arching saber emerged from my hand. I curled my damaged hand against my chest and raised the weapon with my other arm. Heat radiated from the blade. Chute stepped back.

The blade sunk in. The portal swelled. It turned purple. Red. Blue-green-violet-yelloworangeblue. The saber spat back, blasting the evolver from my arm. I landed hard on the frozen ground, jolting the loose bones in my leg. It took several tries to breathe again. The evolver half-folded back into a handle, coughing electrical arcs.

Chute helped me sit up. When I was breathing normally, she asked, "What now?"

Long pause. *"I can, uh, well... I can build another lightning bolt with twice the voltage. The portal won't survive that, but the website might crash."*

"If you crash this website," I said, "won't that release us?"

"Not necessarily. If for some reason it doesn't destroy the portal and crashes the website, you could end up in-between." Another long pause. *"I need to think about this."*

A fire grew from the ground, courtesy of Streeter. Flames crackled off the dry wood, sending up sparks like glowing bugs, which dissolved in the bitter air. Snow began to fall again, dusting the frozen mud.

Chute had that look. Her forehead was tight. Her lips pinched.

"You all right?" I said.

She nodded, rubbed her hands together. We listened to the water fall. "Are we going to get out of here?" she finally asked.

"We'll get out of here."

She spread her hands out toward the flames. She silently debated whether to believe me. There was no reason she should.

"Why do you think he did it?" Chute gestured at the crater.

I thought hard about Broak, with his perfect breeding and his perfect smile. He was a perfect specimen of a human being. But that was the rub: he was still human. He might've had perfect genes, but he'd been raised like a servy. He became just like a mech, following the rules. He was *supposed* to be perfect. But he could not *be* perfect. He was human. Somewhere in his teenage brain he was letting Mom and Dad down. A mom he never had. A dad that never existed.

How could the Paladins be so short-sighted? They were a greater race of humans and they couldn't figure out they'd raised a monster?

"He was a little messed-up in the head," I said. "He was just a kid."

"I don't care, he wasn't good."

"No." I pushed a stick into the fire. "He wasn't."

The fire blazed. The heat stayed right there by the flames, not dispersing into the wintry air. Steam no longer rose from the crater as it slowly filled with snow. It was cold out there. I shook the snow off my head and limped toward Broak.

At the edge of the crater, I held my breath and ignited the evolver. It refused to completely unfold. I squeezed it harder and it finally fused to my arm, shooting sparks in protest. I formed a spade and jabbed at the frozen ground, the blade thumping through it a chunk at a time. Each time I opened the earth with another swing, I cursed the Paladins for creating Broak. I cursed them for their ignorance. Cursed them for what they did to him.

"What're you doing?" Chute said.

"He should be buried."

"I don't think he deserves it. Not after what he did."

I turned to breathe clean air, wiped my eyes. "Maybe."

I didn't know what to think. Broak might've been the leader of the dupes, for all I knew. He might've single-handedly led the human race into extinction had Streeter not roasted him. The Paladins dealt him an impossible life, but where was he supposed to take responsibility? At what point is it his fault and not theirs? In the end, he was just a stupid kid, believed he was the center of the universe, that he was indestructible like all the rest of us.

I mean, it's not like we're born with the manual on how to live life. No one gives us a clue how this is supposed to be done so can any of us be blamed when it all goes wrong? Think about it, we grow up being told there's a fat man dressed in red that lives at the North Pole that gives us presents for free, and if we question the absurdity of it, they tell us we just have to believe and it'll be true. *Are you freaking kidding me?* Reindeer don't fly and jolly fat men don't shove presents down the chimney. But just believe and it'll be true. NO, IT WON'T!

Maybe Broak had the manual to life. He just read it wrong, took it too literal. He wanted life to be perfect and that wasn't possible. Life was perfectly imperfect.

I took another chunk of ground from the shallow grave. No sense deciding on blame. The boy needed a proper burial. Fair or not. The ground thumped again. Chute pried up another piece of the ground with her battle stave. We tossed frozen earth into the crater. The dirt clods were like bricks. We buried him, along with the crawlers, as best we could, then shoveled snow on top when we ran out of earth.

We stood at the lip of the crater, our heads bowed. "God help us all," I said.

Chute laid her head on my shoulder, wrapped her arm around my waist. We let the snow pile on our heads and shoulders until the cold seeped inside.

"Come on," she said. "Let's get back to the fire."

We stayed warm in front of the endless fire, waiting for Streeter to come up with an answer. We didn't talk much. I wished there was something to say so that I could stop thinking about Broak, the way he bubbled in the bottom of the pit. The way he said my name at the end, almost with an edge of final regret. It was so complicated, I just wanted to stop thinking about it, but there wasn't much to say, either. So we sat in silence until a dirt clod rolled off the grave.

I didn't think much of it. It wasn't a big deal. Surprised I even noticed it with the wind howling above the trees, but when the second one tumbled off, I tensed up. I limped around the crater's edge. A jointed stick poked from the fresh snow, feeling the grave like a blind man's cane.

"Streeter!" I hobbled back to Chute.

"What's wrong?" she said.

"Streeter!" I tapped my cheek. "Streeter! Get us out of here!"

All the frozen clods rumbled. A seven-legged crawler stood, legs kinked and wobbly. It fell to one side, tried to stand again. Its scarred body undulated. The burn wounds and deep gashes sealed. It was healing.

"The crawlers, Streeter! They survived!"

SNOWDEAF

A second crawler rose up from the grave, its body pulsing. The evolver unfolded onto my arm, but it was sputtering. I summoned hot whips, I'd lash the things to pieces, but a weak flame only flickered in my hand.

"You guys need to run," Streeter said.

"Are you out of your freaking mind?" I shouted. "My leg doesn't work! You need to build us something... a transporter, a cruiser, anything!"

"I'm busy with the lightning, I can't do it all!"

"If we don't get out of here, LIGHTNING WON'T MATTER!"

A third crawler squirmed, running in a circle like a fly with one wing.

Chute shoved the portal into her pouch and slid her arm around me. "We have to try."

We headed past the cave and into the trees. Each step throbbed with agony, and I was panting after only a few yards. There was a narrow trail winding uphill. The going was easier, but the pain worse. Behind us, the crawlers screeched, weaker than before the lightning strike, but at just the right pitch to twist my nerves.

"I can't." I covered my face. "I can't... I can't do this..."

"STREETER! GET US SOMETHING NOW!" Chute shouted at him like he was a god looking over a forsaken world.

"Come on, you can do this," she urged me in a softer voice.

"I can't, Chute." I turned so she wouldn't see my face. "It just... it hurts too much."

"You don't have a choice."

"I'm only going to slow you down."

"I'm not leaving you here, Socket Greeny!" She placed both hands on my face and forced me to look at her. "I'm never leaving you, so if you want to save me, you got to save yourself."

Her cheeks flamed red. The *look* was gone—the worried look—replaced by steely courage. I couldn't move and deadly spiders screeched behind us, but all I wanted at that moment was to kiss her on the lips.

She held out her hand, and hoisted me up, hip to hip, and together we started up the path. I closed my eyes, searching for strength to match what I'd seen in her eyes. The spark grew brighter, the power centers of my awakening whirring along my spine. If it would work, if I could stop time, I could save us.

Metal clashed as the space in front of us twisted and warped. If a crawler was materializing before us, there was no use running. We watched something assemble from empty space. Pieces sprang from the air, clinging together

214

as more pieces emerged, rolling, turning, and clicking into place until a round platform hovered inches off the ground.

"It's all I can do," Streeter said. *"Take the jetter and go. They're on the move."*

"It's enough," Chute said. "I can get us miles away before they get this far."

She helped me onto the back edge of the jetter and climbed onto the front. I wrapped my good arm around her waist and lay my chin on her shoulder. The jetter sagged under our weight.

"Go to the tundra," Streeter said. *"There's a power dome that will protect you. It's indestructible. Once you're in, nothing can touch you."*

"Tundra?" I said. "Build it right here, Streeter, right in front of us! We don't have time to get to the—"

"JUST GET TO THE GODDAMN TUNDRA! I can't build it right in front of you. It's complex code, I don't have time to build it from scratch!"

The jetter hummed loudly, lifted and surged forward. Chute tossed her lookits and followed them. The sharp wind blurred my sight. My inner ears ached, but Streeter's voice, calmer, sounded clear in my head.

"The power dome is remnant code from an earlier battle on the tundra, that's the best I can do." Screeches blasted from all around. *"So please... just get to the tundra."*

Chute leaned forward and pushed the jetter at top speed. How could she see? Her hair whipped my face and I clung to her tightly. We reached the top of the ridge and followed a sloping path to the left, gently slaloming left and right.

A lookit returned. "We're going into the trees," she shouted back. "It's the quickest way!"

The forest was dark and dense. The going got slow. We painfully bumped trees, stumps and logs. I squeezed tighter. The forest rumbled. Tremors traveled deep underground.

They were coming.

I didn't need to say it. She heard it, too. *Go faster.* If we hit a tree and damaged the jetter, it was over. Streeter didn't have time to build another. *But still, go faster.*

Up ahead, the shadows gave way. Light poked through the impenetrable forest. "We're almost there!" she shouted.

We leaned into a tight turn and ducked beneath a low branch. The crude path widened beyond the last turn. Chute took the corner tight, caught a twisting vine hidden in a snow drift. The jetter turned a full circle, tipped back, and couldn't right itself.

A bell rang.

It was ringing in the darkness.

Something picked me up. Shook me.

"Get up, Socket!" a voice said. "Don't quit on me! It's right there... It's—"

It wasn't so bad, where I was. I didn't know where that was, but it wasn't so bad. Maybe a little chilly. I couldn't see in the pitch black, but at least it didn't hurt.

Where am I? Wasn't I supposed to be doing something? We were trying to get... something... or somewhere. *We?*

A light twittered, like a lighthouse beacon going round and round. It was sparkly. I urged myself closer to it. It was curious and bright. It wanted something. The next time it came around it glared like the sun. I tried to look away before it burned out my eyes, but it was impossible. I had no eyelids. The light was everywhere. I wanted to run and hide, to sleep. The light refused to let me.

It rushed into me. Filled me.

Power centers burst to life and energy surged. I had a body but I wasn't in it. It was broken. I saw my shattered knee and, with a thought, healed it. The bones and cartilage fused together as good as new. The wrist was damaged, too. I commanded it to reassemble. Nerves repaired. Muscles healed.

I am awake.

In a single thought, I returned to my renewed body. Cold tightened my skin and took my breath. Time was not moving. Motionless snowflakes glittered like diamonds in the air. The waning sun cast an iridescent shine on the snowdrifts, like ocean waves in moonlight. Chute was crouched over me—stuck in time—her face turned to the sky, mouth open, about to cry for help or curse our fate. Jagged energy enveloped her.

A yellow dome, like a vibrant igloo, squatted in the snowdrifts on the far side of the tundra a thousand feet away. I wouldn't be able to timeslice forever; weakness had already entered my legs as the timeslicing metabolism devoured me. I had to get to the power dome, had to squeeze every second out of the spark that I could. The crawlers weren't far behind.

I picked up Chute and started over the white desert, carving through the waist-deep drifts, hopping when the snow was over my knees. Snowflakes bounced off my face. Snot ran over my lips. Chute got heavier.

Halfway there, I began to quiver. How far could I push it before my body was sucked dry? *As far as I could.* I plowed onward, going around the deepest drifts. Exhausted and numb, Chute slipped. I tumbled over her.

The dying sun brightened. Snowflakes jolted sideways. A breeze washed over me.

The dome was fifty yards away. I could do it. I picked her up and started up the deepest drift yet. My breath streamed out in a long cloud. I blinked several times to focus. The drift ended abruptly and we went down again. So numb, my legs were nothing. Gravity intensified. I tried to lift her, but couldn't get her past my knees. The world quaked.

Can't do it.

The timeslicing spark slipped from my grip. The wind sheared the feeling from my face. Snowflakes struck like rocks. Chute sat up, dazed. I took her hand and tried to lift her. "The dome... we're almost there."

She understood and helped me up. I pretended to run but could barely throw one leg in front of the other. We fell again. She shouted, but the wind blasted her words away. I started to crawl. She tried to pick me up.

Trees exploded on the far side and crawlers blasted onto the tundra like galloping creatures from another planet on twitching legs, their stride distorted by missing limbs. The pitch of their screeching was perfect. It made the gale force wind seem like a summer breeze, slamming our nervous systems, cutting away any strength we had left. We dropped like the dead.

The sky swirled darkly over us. Lightning crackled in the clouds but did not come down.

Scccreeeeeeeeeee!

The portal slipped from Chute's pouch. I took it and crawled. Chute was next to me, her ragged hair hanging over her face.

A shadow passed over us.

Snow exploded around my forearm and the portal rolled out of my hand.

The crawlers stepped over me. I pushed up and collapsed again. A gash from my elbow to my wrist flapped open, exposing bones and spilling blood. The snow was sprayed red

This is the Internet. This is not the skin. THIS IS NOT REAL!

I tried to run but my legs only kicked. Tried to roll. Tried to scream. It was too much too much. TOO MUCH!

A crawler hovered inches from my face, stinking of burning circuits and baked clay. Its faceless body pressed its sticky body against my cheek and quivered like it was sniffing. Another one wobbled over Chute while a third one bobbed between us, waiting its turn.

It lifted off me, undulating like a thinking brain. A hole opened on its belly, black and bottomless. It screeched, but I didn't hear it. My eardrums immediately burst. In silence, I convulsed.

In darkness, I screamed.

My sight returned. The crawler limped away, swaying in the silent wind towards Chute to have a turn with her. The third one stooped over me and pressed against my cheek.

My eyes wanted to close but I refused to let them. Chute was limp. I reached for her. I couldn't let them kill her. I could not let this happen. I forced myself to move, but the crawler corralled my hand, placed it gently on my chest. It pressed against my severed arm, came up with a splotch of blood on its belly, absorbing the stain. It turned pale, looked to the others. Undulated. They abandoned Chute. She remained still.

They gathered around me, lifting me with their twiggy legs. They spread my arms, held my legs together. They'd found me. I was the one to pull apart. I was the one they would decode. They would integrate me into their database and I would become one of them. They would put me inside the duplications. I would become the living dead.

Mission accomplished.

Two crawlers held me while the third one, slightly larger, pressed against me. It wrapped its round body around me, warm and sticky. My cells began to dissolve, liquefying as the world faded.

Gray became darkness.

Would I go to the in-between, or would I just go to sleep, never to wake? Would I awaken as one of them—see the iron rule of duplicated humans for centuries to come? Would I experience every cry, every plea, to make them stop? Or would I see the human race follow them like lemmings?

The time spark beat somewhere inside. It was the only thing I could feel, thumping in my awareness. There was little left of me now. If I took the spark, I would empty my body. The timeslice would suck out the last drop of life.

I clenched my hands and sliced it anyway.

I would slice time to the end.

RIPPED

I slid out of the crawler's snotty grip and stared into its maw. What was left of my clothes was covered in slime. The thick mucus kept me from freezing.

The portal had rolled inside the dome. My grip on time was already slipping. I didn't have much left. Life was fading. I would die in the timeslice and disappear from the world. I would die so the crawler wouldn't absorb me. Die before they could integrate me.

Chute. I couldn't leave her. I rolled for her, just to touch her. There had to be something I could do. There had to be an answer. I held her head firmly against my chest and wrapped my legs around her waist, trying to crawl to the safety of the dome. But I didn't have the strength to even do that.

I need help! I cried. The words drifted silently from me. No one would hear my plea. Not even me.

I convulsed again. The ground trembled.

Time stood still, but the world shook. The sky tore open, revealing a bright red slice through the dreary clouds. I felt the ripping in my chest.

The website was crashing. A crevasse opened at the far end of the tundra, swallowing snow into a deadly void of random data. It traveled across the tundra slowly, widening and inhaling the environment. Snow rushed across the plain. The forest bordering the wide tundra bent under its force. Sticks, leaves, rocks, rabbits... all of it was sucked into the rip.

It would reach us and suck us in as it split the tundra. My evolver belched but unfolded around my good arm. I summoned a whip that fell short of the dome. I cursed, pulling it back. I closed my eyes, imagining the longest whip possible then let it fly. It lashed out, slightly brighter, slightly thinner, and long enough to wrap around the base of an ancient spruce.

My grip on time slipped before I passed out. Snowflakes jittered and danced. The wind returned, driving snow over the tundra that curved like breaking waves under the voracious appetite of the rip. The tundra had split open, the rip halfway to us. The horizon was nearly gone. The details of trees and mountains had dissolved.

The website was going down and nothing would stop it. In deafness, the destruction was eerily silent. The forest began to shake as the rip widened. The portal bounced against the dome, trapped inside its protective barrier. The evolver whip grew taut as I was drawn toward the approaching chasm. The crawler stood tall, scanning the environment. It took only seconds to analyze the situation. Seconds they didn't have. The rip gained speed, raced past us and into the trees, sucking up branches and snow. The two smaller crawlers leaped, but the rip vacuumed them down. They hit the ground, their spindly legs scratching the frozen ground as they bounced over the edge. Down they went. Forever.

The third crawler anchored into the ground, fighting the rip's force. The first of the large branches bounced past. The evolver whip stretched. The force was too great. We slid toward the encroaching abyss.

The crawler slid, too, etching tracks in the permafrost. I grabbed the lash with my other arm, the wind blowing the wound open, the skin flapping. The crawler jabbed at me with one leg, impaling the ground inches from my ribs. It lost its hold, slid faster, flopping over the edge, desperately hanging on.

I clutched Chute between my legs. I could feel nothing. The evolver lash stretched thinner. The rip was closer and the vacuum stronger. My legs fell over the edge. Chute dangled inside. Below, the void was colorless, depthless, and dimensionless. She was slipping. I hooked my wounded arm around her.

The entire horizon was fuzzy gray static. The data was gone. The ground near us rushed overhead, curling like carpet on its way to chaos and randomness. My knees had slipped under Chute's armpits as we twisted on the end of the line. The crawler's red eyelight rolled around its body and focused on me. It teetered on the very edge.

The lash flickered. The evolver started unfolding. I grabbed for the slippery ledge, slipping deeper. Chute's legs faded in the void's depth. The evolver fell off my arm, rolled past me, dissolving below into millions of specks.

We didn't fall.

Something was latched onto my wrist.

There, bent over the edge, was a shadowy arm, its fingers locked around my arm. A head and torso looked down at us. The shadow returned.

Pivot! You came for us!

Another shadowy arm clung to Chute, her body turning in the wind. He held us there. He didn't pull us up, he just held us.

[I have you, Master Socket.]

Spindle?

Trees vaporized in the void's depth. The crawler slashed at us one last time, slipped off the ledge and dissolved into nothingness.

We twisted helplessly as the rip crept beneath the dome that slid down like electrical gel. The portal stuck to the side of the wall, oozing like molasses. It picked up speed, the colors bright and glowing. It broke free, shot down into the ravenous void.

The explosion was silent. Bright, like that of a dying star.

The light consumed us.

No cold. No pain.

In-between.

I was in the dark in-between. Bodiless. Pure awareness.

There was something different, this time. Another awareness floated with me. A familiar presence.

Spindle?

There was movement.

[Yes, Master Socket.]

Spindle! I thought you were Pivot! I thought this whole time Pivot was the shadow!

[I am the one that assumed the form of a shadow. Not Master Pivot.]

It was you... My thoughts rang like words. *Am I... am I dead?*

[You are not dead. You will return to your body when it is ready.]

Which body?

[Your skin, of course. The portal was destroyed, releasing you from the sim.]

224

The darkness moved again. It hummed. I felt it at my core.

You saved me, Spindle.

[Your father saved you.]

My father?

[He imbedded a secret code in my processor. When the time was right, I came to you as the shadow and activated your powers. And when you needed me, I came to your aid.]

He told me on the day I first arrived at the Garrison that he was programmed to assist me. And that's why the shadow felt so familiar, why he felt like my father. Even in death, my father was there.

Why did you wait so long?

[Despite what you believe, you did not need me.]

The darkness hummed stronger and deeper. I was moving.

The Paladins will know what you did, Spindle. They'll shut you down completely this time. I won't see you when I return, will I?

[Master Pivot seems to think they will not shut me down.]

Pivot came back?

[He never left.]

But... the Paladins will imprison him this time. They can't see the future, they'll never let him leave again.

[The Paladins could never stop Master Pivot from leaving. They have always known that. He stayed in the Preserve of his own volition. After taking you to awaken, he decided it was time to leave.]

Where did he go?

[Missing, Master Socket. He went missing. They will not find him. But he can always be found if you need him.]

The darkness swirled this time. The hum was closer. It hurt nowhere specific. It just hurt.

Pivot loved my father.

[Indeed, he did. Without him, I could not have come for you.]

Pain lanced through me, up and down and side-to-side. Something thumped in rhythm. Pain focalized in several spots throughout the darkness.

I was returning.

Chute and Streeter. I almost forgot! *Are they all right?*

I moved faster. Noise was coming.

Spindle! Where are you? Tell me, are they all right? ARE THEY ALL RIGHT?

The pain returned in full force.

Muffled sounds. Chairs and tables were turned over and shoved aside. Muted voices shouted.

"Three kids, two boys and one girl. About sixteen years old."

"Sir, this one's the Greeny boy. Alert the Commander."

"Get the EMT here immediately. Set up a secure perimeter. I don't want to see lookits within a hundred yards. Clear the room!"

There were tables. A ceiling. It was a room. A *real* one.

"I need three reconstitution IVs on the Greeny kid immediately," a woman shouted. Her fingers pressed on my neck. "Weak pulse."

"How's he alive?" someone else muttered.

I was on my back. The lights were dim. People were now everywhere, looking down at me. Three of them were dressed in black. The Paladins. They were right there in plain sight of everyone.

"The girl's in shock," the woman said.

"Get the minders in here to stabilize her." One of the Paladins squatted next to me. The emergency worker stared at him.

"Who the hell are you?" she said.

The Paladin didn't acknowledge her. He put his hand over my head and a healing warmth oozed through me. He slapped a patch on my neck and strength leached into my body.

"What did you just do to him?" The emergency worker was about to call for assistance, but then the Paladin looked at her, *thought* at her, and she stopped.

More EMTs burst into the room, called more orders and hovered over me. A warm, soft presence crawled from the back of my neck and slithered down the back of my shirt. Rudder hid inside my sweatshirt from the EMTs' poking and prodding. I could feel his purring against my stomach and how it radiated through me.

"You did it, Socket." Streeter grabbed my shoulder; his voice seemed so far away.

His face was slack, but he was smiling. My arm was skinny, like the muscle had been sucked out. My cheeks hung. Big hands pulled Streeter away, rolled him onto his back, but he was still smiling. His mouth moved. *You did it.*

There must've been ten people over me. I could barely see the ceiling anymore. They strapped gear around my arms, attached things to my neck and chest, holding up bags, squeezing fluid into my veins. The Paladin put another patch on the other side of my neck. I couldn't feel my left arm, but it was there. No bone, no blood. I wiggled my fingers. A woman shoved my arm back down.

"Where's Chute?" My voice echoed in my head. I had the feeling I was shouting, but I could barely hear it. "Streeter, where's Chute?"

"I need a heart regulator," some guy said. "Pre-sets will work for now, but activate the nervous relay, we need to decompress their nervous systems immediately."

"Where is she?" I tried to shove them out of the way. "Where's Chute?"

The lady put my arms down, again. I didn't have the strength to break her grip. I looked side-to-side. There were too many of them. I couldn't even see Streeter anymore.

"I need that regulator over here, now!" the guy shouted again, to my left.

I tried to look between their legs. I arched my back and shouted, "CHUTE! WHERE ARE YOU?"

"Relax, son." The lady put her hand on my forehead. "We're going to get you out of here—"

"No, no, no…" I shook her off. "I'm not going, not until you show me where she is…"

A thin finger hooked around my finger, squeezed softly. The woman squatted to my right, wrapping a band around my elbow. She stood, shouted to others coming into the room, moved out of the way and revealed Chute's exhausted face and her arm reaching out to me. Her finger hooked around mine.

"I'm right here, Socket." Chute smiled, weakly. Blinked heavily.

We got out.

Chute didn't let go, her arm sticking through a gap between boots. They lifted the stretcher. More shouts. More commands. A woman's face hovered over mine. She put something on my forehead and I was suddenly sleepy. They moved me from the room. I couldn't remember letting go of Chute.

FISHING

I was on a beach. The sand was hot and dry and pushed between my toes. I dug my feet down to cooler, damper sand below. The beach appeared to extend for miles in both directions. A ship sailed on the horizon with shrimp nets hanging from the sides. The orange sun reflected off the small waves. Dolphins looped on the surface, blowing showers near the beach where fiddler crabs raced foamy waves.

In reality, I was in a small room. If I tried to dip my toes in the water I'd kick the wall. Just another illusion. Those tricky Paladins.

They put me to sleep after I was evacuated from the school. They kept me like that for a month. They filled me with medicine and liquid food. I had the puncture wounds in my arm to prove it. Their gear decompressed my nervous system so I could hear again, so I would believe my arm wasn't actually split open by an artificial spider on a snowy tundra. They kept me on that cot and servys tended my injuries while Paladins stood over my comatose body, tapping their chins, murmuring about my future. Their future. Humanity's future. Mostly they thought to each other so I wouldn't hear them, but I heard their thoughts when I came close to waking.

Sometimes I heard them come in and out of the room. I could smell them. I smelled jasmine most often. *Mom.* Quite often, she would sit on the edge of my bed and push back my hair. Then I'd fade again, back to the painless void of sleep. That's when the minders would come, penetrating me when I was least present, picking through my memories like looters, piecing together the events of the Rime. When they had everything they wanted, that's when they let me wake.

They wouldn't let me out of the room, for observational purposes. But after a day, it was suffocating, so they started up the simulated environment scenery. One morning I'd wake up in the desert, the next I'm at the top of Niagara Falls. This morning, good ole Charleston, South Carolina. All I could do was stand there and watch, smell and listen.

"What scene would you like tomorrow?" a servy asked.

"I want out of here."

"I am sorry, please repeat your request. What scene would you like?" Like it couldn't understand why I'd want to leave the Garrison.

This morning, the third morning, a leaper shuddered. Mom walked into the room. Her steps landed slowly. She watched the waves wash ashore. The shrimp boat cast its nets. Her expression was stoic, but her energy jittered between waves of hardness and softness. She was not accustomed to feeling what she was feeling right then. It wasn't often she experienced the depth of fear like she had in the past month, not since my father had died. And nor had she experienced this kind of relief when she saw me standing there, alive and well. "My son," she whispered.

She didn't hug me or weep, but the energy around her was soaked with salty flavors. Her hands were quivering. *[Allow me a moment of weakness,]* she thought to me or whoever was tuning in.

She dropped her head and walked closer to the water. The crabs scattered like she might step on them. We watched the sun get closer to the horizon and the shrimp boats sailed out of view. When she was composed, she said, "When your father died, they wanted me to quit."

She tucked her hair behind her ear.

"They said it would be too difficult for me to stay and watch you awaken. It would be too difficult to make sound decisions instead of emotional ones. They said I would only interfere and, in the end, I would harm you. I had to choose." Her voice faltered. "To be a mother or a leader."

She wiped her nose, folded her arms. No moody, this time.

"The best way to help you, to be whatever mother I could be, was to stay. To be here when you awakened. I knew you would hate me for it, but life demanded it."

Her emotions flailed around her. It took all her strength to allow them to thrash without overwhelming her into another moment of weakness. But she was losing that battle.

"It has been harder... to watch you suffer... then I ever could've imagined."

My heart thumped in time with hers. I stepped next to her. Like a magnet grabbing a metal rod, she put her arms around me. When was the last time she'd hugged me? It had been too long.

"Forgive me," she said.

Her eyes were wet, but not a single tear fell. My senses heightened. I smelled her fragrance, heard the leapers creep above and below us, felt the minders in nearby rooms

231

watching our thoughts. I had awakened. Somehow, her embrace awakened me even further and her saltiness seeped into my awareness. It settled in my throat and swelled behind my eyes. All that anger I reserved for her had vanished.

"Your father…"

"Would be proud," I said.

She smiled, half laughed. She was shaking.

"Thank you," I said.

She pressed the back of my hands to her eyes and let go. She stepped back and calmed her breathing. Her emotions, once white-capped waves, settled glassy and calm. Her Paladin nature was back in control, although I could now see Mother there, too.

"As you may have guessed," she said, "the Paladin Nation is no longer covert. The past month has forced us into the public eye. The world now knows of our existence."

"So the world survived?" I said.

"The war is over. The duplication population has been eliminated."

"What about Streeter and Chute?"

"Their parents are with them, here in the Garrison."

"When can I see them?"

"They're still recovering."

"Still recovering?" I fidgeted. "What's that mean?"

"It's nothing to worry about. Streeter is undergoing precautionary mental decompression. Chute sustained more serious injuries."

"She's going to be all right." My chest fluttered. "Right?"

"She going to be fine, it's just taking longer than anticipated. The doctors don't want to rush her recovery; they're allowing her nervous system time to reconnect to her body. The awareness transference she experienced was quite traumatic. Her physical brain activity had stopped for over an hour."

"I recovered just fine."

She squeezed my forearm. "You're not like her."

Not anymore.

"Is Broak dead?" I asked.

"You're not responsible for his death. Neither is Streeter. Broak had been corrupted."

Like a computer. "The Paladins are just as much at fault," I said. "They manufactured him like a weapon."

"Broak was responsible for his own actions. He chose to betray the Paladin Nation. To betray the human race."

"They raised him like a machine. No wonder he went to them."

Her upper lip tightened. "Broak will not receive my pity."

She was not taking any more questions on that topic. That was that. Broak was dead. Life is such.

"What about Pivot?" I asked.

"It was time for him to go missing. The Paladins were going to take him inside and set every minder in the Nation on him, although I'm not convinced that would've worked. But I don't think that's why he left. He watched out for you while you were here. Somehow, I think that was his mission."

"Tell me what it means when he's missing?"

"He has the ability to make others... not see him. He could be right in front of you, yet convince you not to see him. His powers are beyond comprehension. I don't think I need to convince you of that."

"He's got to come back."

I almost said *I need him.* It's what I meant. Mom thought for a moment, softly touched my cheek. She let her Paladin mode slip to show me the sadness that rested in her soul, the sadness of my father's death and how she carried that with her every day. She let me know that I, too, carried that sadness, whether I knew it or not. My father is gone. So is Pivot.

Life is such.

A door appeared to open in mid-air between two swaying palm trees. She was done. No more about Pivot, or my father or Broak. She was leaving. But I wanted more. I wrapped my mind around her to uncover her thoughts, to spill what she knew against her will.

"Stop." Her mind tightened, guarding her thoughts that, seconds earlier, she allowed me to see. She didn't have the strength to hold me out, but bristled like a cat that wouldn't go down without a fight. "Don't look inside me, Socket. Stealing thoughts is not something you can do whenever you want."

I pulled back. She smoothed non-existent wrinkles on her jacket. "You have a lot to learn about the mental realm."

She left the room. Her fragrance lingered. Another shrimp boat sailed in from the right.

THE PEBBLE

I was still kept in the room, promised that it would be soon when they let me get out. I spent a lot of time contemplating what had happened, and what would happen, but I was getting tired of thinking. And I was tired of shrimpers throwing their nets into the sea.

I called for news reports in the Charleston area. A holographic man and woman appeared at a desk with sea foam swirling around their feet.

"More information is being released about the Paladin Nation," the woman said with a reporter's dramatic flair. "A representative is scheduled to speak to the public. How long have they been in existence? How are they funded? Why are they secret? These are just some of the questions global leaders want answered."

"It's the classic movie *Men in Black*," the man said.

"It certainly is." She smiled at him. "And the public is responding."

The reporters disappeared, replaced by an angry mob, smaller in scale. Hundreds waved signs, shouting things like *Justice* and *Freedom of Information.* Several spoke to an interviewer.

"The Paladins need to be accountable." A balding man stood before me with his arms stiffly at his sides. "They are not above the law. The secrecy is an outrage. I don't care if they're fighting aliens, man-eating tigers or the wicked witch—we demand full disclosure!" He pounded his fist into his other hand. "A society that keeps secrets has something to hide!"

"While the initial reaction is mostly outrage," the woman spoke as protesters continued to march, "Paladins are reluctant to disclose much. The question everyone is asking is whether we would know anything at all if multiple attacks had not taken place around the world, one of which occurred at a local high school."

"That's right," the male reporter chipped in. "Little information has been released since it was left in ruins."

An aerial view of the school appeared. The dome roof of the Pit was gone, so were the seats and the floor. The tagghet field was littered with the bleachers.

"We're not even sure who or what attacked," the man said. "There appears to be some sort of machinery that emerged from an explosion and local authorities want to know who is responsible. It is thought the attackers were targeting the school's virtualmode portal, one of the most powerful in the state that also lacked sufficient security, but what they would do with it is unknown."

The grainy footage hovered around the parking lot but the thick smoke obscured much of the view. Occasionally, jointed legs poked out as the Paladins' weapons flared blue from the ground, leaving remains of the crawlers twitching on the asphalt.

236

"What you may not know is that some believe children had something to do with stopping the attack. Emergency workers reported three teenagers were found in a remote virtualmode lab. They were in very poor condition but they were not able to explain why since the Paladins on site quickly took them away."

The view switched to Buxbee's lab. The Paladins hustled three stretchers into a large black vehicle. The emergency workers are swarming around them but not able to do anything about it.

"However, the Paladins refuse to identify the youths or reveal what they were doing during the attack."

The images dissolved into the sand. "The Authority requests your presence," the room said. "Formal attire is required. A leaper will arrive in five minutes."

With the illusion gone, the room was white and ordinary again and claustrophobia was quickly falling around me like a straight jacket.

A suit emerged from the wall, hanging on a hook, plum colored with mustard trim. The pants were loose-fitting, the overcoat hung nicely, although the shoulders were a bit square. The shoes were square and clunky. I stripped down, dressed and waited for the leaper to open, leaving the shoes on the bed.

There was no escort. I tried not to think where Spindle was. I stepped inside and was transported to the same room I met the Authority the last time. Mom and Commander Diggs were on my right. Pike and his minder assistants were in front of me. Broak, of course, was not there.

The room flowed with unseen currents. It was thicker than electricity, more like cream. The mental realm. Psychic energy emanated from the Commander, shining like an organic power plant, and Mom, less so. Thoughts and energy beamed in from around the world, from all those watching this event, peeping in through unseen lookits embedded in the moldable walls.

The minders, however, did not shine. They were dark vortices sucking energy back, holding their thoughts at guard against probing minds. They were impenetrable psychic giants, the ability to pry a mind in half like a walnut or close theirs like a 200-cube encrypted vault. They stood motionless, staring ahead through black wrapped glasses. Their nostrils flared, smelling me. Their dimness lightened like they were tempted to open for a look into my mind, although there was nothing new for them to see.

I walked to a bright spot on the floor. The circular wall rose fiercely. The figureheads were seated and staring. New energy swarmed around the large room of subtle pinks, reds and violets. Each color exuded a different flavor. I let my mind experience the silky flow of their essence. Some were coarse, some fine. All of it luminescent, except for the minders. Their essence was forbidding, dark and gritty. Not like sand paper, but like a rock in my shoe or something stuck between my teeth. Something like a pebble they held, a fine grain of sand, solid and dense. Something they held secret from the rest of us.

"Hearing 24489 of Socket Pablo Greeny," a bodiless woman said, "is now in session."

"Right." The Authority, with his beefy jowls and tired eyes, looked down on me. "No need to make this lengthy. You have been accepted into the Paladin Nation, Socket Greeny."

Mom released a long-held breath. I was not surprised. Was anyone? But I surprised myself, and everyone else, when a question emerged. "What if I don't want to be one?"

Tense emotions rippled amongst the counsel and the luminescence dimmed. Had no one ever asked that question? He wasn't asking me, he was telling me I was accepted. Now I wasn't so sure I wanted in this club. The

Authority laughed like a coughing dog, his cheeks jiggling. The mounting tension broke.

"Every man and woman has a choice, of course! We are not captors, Socket Greeny. We fight for freedom so that every person has the opportunity to answer a question like that for themselves. It is a great opportunity to see what you are, but, more so, have the courage to be it. There are many people that see the tremendous potential inside you, but I cannot tell you what that is. Nor can your mother or anyone else. *You* have to see it for yourself. Only *you* can become it."

I could refuse to be one of them, just like he said. Walk out of that room and leave it all behind. Go back to the house, call on the television and kick back with a plate full of nachos. But life couldn't go back, not like it was before. No matter what he said, there was no going back no matter how much I wanted to, no matter how much I tried. I had awakened. There was no changing that anymore than I could become a baby sucking my thumb. I had seen my true nature. How could I be anything else?

Sometimes life doesn't ask for it to happen. It demands.

The Authority nodded, sensing the resolution and acceptance of my thoughts. He had my answer. I saw. *I am a Paladin.* He looked down at his notes.

"You are untrained, Socket Greeny," he said. "You have recently awakened with little more than instinct to guide you. I can only imagine what kind of Paladin you will be once fully developed. The world will be a better place, a safer place, once you have."

His big belly pushed out beneath his hanging robe when he stood. He began to clap his thick hands. The walloping sound shook the room.

"Congratulations." A tiny smile broke across his droopy face. "And bravo."

One after another, the members stood at the top of the wall and clapped like thunder. Not all of them, though.

Several remained seated, their hands planted firmly on their laps. The minders didn't move. They didn't frown, scowl or glare. And the annoying pebble was more noticeable.

I opened my mind to the room, absorbed all the energy, all the thoughts, colors and essence. I opened to the happiness and bitterness and the full range of emotions. I had nothing to hide; they could look into my mind all they wanted. I was fully open, fully aware and fully present. My awareness washed over everything, including the pebble. It took shape. I experienced its size, texture and hardness. It was a distinct object, a substantial container of thoughts. It contained information. And it had a location. The minders weren't holding the pebble. It was Pike.

The Authority held his arms out and silenced the applause. The ones standing remained standing. He paused, allowing silence to settle. The Authority tipped his head. "Your duty is to serve, Socket Greeny," he said, "to your utmost."

I have to be quick for all to see.

The walls trembled and began to sink. The images of the Authority and his cohorts shriveled. Their essence became chaotic, drawing back through their projected, shrinking images as their awareness sought to return to their skin somewhere in the world.

I summoned all my psychic energy and gathered it like an arrow with an indestructible tip. I pulled back the string, filled the arrow with tension and fired it, with every thought, every bit of strength I had. All my essence drained into that shot. I was depleted, fell on my knees, and almost passed out. It took the minders by surprise, bored through their mental walls before they could throw themselves against it. The arrow spiked Pike's mind like an icy sliver. Pierced the hidden pebble.

Penetrated it.

It burst with a million colors. Endless thoughts sprang from the pebble and filled the room for all to see. The thoughts he hid from his assistant minders. The thoughts he carefully tucked inside the pebble to make himself forget so that none would know he was hiding them. The thoughts he couldn't dare let anyone know. The ones that would break his mission. Crush his existence.

He had sabotaged Broak's lessons, exposed his human pain; convinced him there was a better way. The Paladins could not be trusted, look what they were doing to him. They were dirty. Imperfect. Mortal. There was a better way, Broak. One you were meant for. Join me. To make a better world. A perfect world.

Pike was still human but he was a spy. *He was Broak's mentor.*

A second did not pass in normal time. I barely raised my head to see the wall spit back out of the floor. The Authority and his minions' eyes bulged with surprise. They heard the hidden thoughts. They understood. A SPY? IN OUR SANCTUARY?

The assistant minders comprehended immediately. They turned on Pike and corralled his poisonous thoughts before he counterattacked with a psychic arrow of his own, one that would turn my brain into grits. They saved me from his mind, but could not hold him. It took a tenth of a second for Pike to disappear into a timeslice, like slipping through a fissure in the fabric of space-time.

He reappeared, in that same instance, a step in front of me, his lethal fingers aimed for my windpipe. His strike—centimeters from my neck—was stopped short by three crawler guards. They popped out of a timeslice and loomed over us, their jointed legs anchored like steel bars. Silky strands wrapped around his legs and arms. They were watching, slicing time when Pike sliced. This time, the spiders saved me.

The room sizzled with essence. Warnings flew. Alerts commanded. The crawlers wrapped Pike tighter. The minders strained to control his mind. His thoughts seeped through their containment like fibrous roots, crackling after me. He pried through my weakened psychic defense. I leaned back, but space was no match for the cold tips of his sharp mind that squeezed inside. He slithered behind my eyeballs. I couldn't stop him.

More minders entered the room. They circled him like blind men, gave support to the struggling assistants. The icy tentacles slowly pulled out of me. They sealed him inside their psychic prison. Pike struggled, spit bubbling on his lips. He cursed, tossing his head around to break the containment.

There were shouts. ORDER! ORDER! More crawlers entered, poking their legs between us, hovering over us, their eyelights ominously directed at Pike. The Commander directed traffic. Doors opened along the walls. Mom rushed me to an open leaper. The crawlers had Pike cocooned, knocking his glasses from his face. His white eyeballs looked in my direction. Blood vessels branched like lightning across them in one last effort. Minders stepped between us.

The leaper closed.

I would've crumpled on the floor had Mom not held me. "They continue to underestimate you," she said.

SPIDER WEBS

The Garrison was structured and suffocating. A tomb. They sent Pike to a remote prison for debriefing somewhere in the world where few people knew. It might've been a thousand feet below ground, might've been in space. No one was going to get to him and he wasn't getting to anyone. A team of minders were assigned to him around the clock, scouring his mind for every memory, every thought, that would expose every instance of deception. He was not a duplicate, he was human. *But is the battle really over?*

What did I get in return for exposing the world's most dangerous spy? Tests, that's what I got. No reward. No vacation. I got tests. Five days later, they sent a guy to my room. "Would you like to go to the Preserve?"

Um. Yes.

Long-necked birds glided over the treetops, finding bare branches to rest. I stood inside the entrance and breathed deep the flow of Mother Earth. Weeds sprouted along the trail leading to the banyan tree. Swards of grass and tropical palms lined the shrinking path. Great big leaves hung in the way, dripping condensation. Banana spiders built intricate, dewy webs across the path and perched in the center waiting the next victim. I wandered down the slope and knelt in front of the first web. The enormous spider, white and yellow, walked in circles and dropped her abdomen on each strand to repair holes from an earlier kill. Her long legs navigated the deathtrap with ease, pulling the web tighter and deadlier. Only she could walk the web without getting tangled.

I scooped up a handful of soil, let it trickle between my fingers. I could stay in the Preserve as long as I liked, the guy said. Just let us know when you're ready to come back inside. But that would never happen and they knew that. They wanted another Pivot. They were betting on me.

A zebra butterfly hit the outside of the web. The spider stopped, felt the vibrations. I plucked the butterfly from the web. It perched on my finger, wagged its black-and-white-striped wings and lifted off in a safer direction.

The leaper vibrated back at the entrance. I sifted another handful of soil. Footsteps softly approached from behind. Bare feet stopped next to my pile of dirt. Mechanical tendons stretched under the supple, silver skin. I looked up at the wavering plum overcoat and the faceplate that reflected the forest greens and orange sunrise.

Spindle. *He's alive.*

I held my excitement in check, not wanting to spoil the moment. He was there, giving pause to the morning. I smiled to myself, knocking the dirt off my hands. "Where have you been?"

"They have been testing me, Master Socket," he said. "Much like you."

"What'd they find?"

"They discovered your father's programming. They looked for more but did not find any."

His chest expanded as if he took a deep breath. I squeezed his bulging bicep, smacked his back. I wanted to hug him, but that would've been stupid, hugging an android. Right?

"I'm really glad to see you, Spindle."

"And I am happy to see you, Master Socket." He bowed, slightly. "You have been a joy to serve."

"Happy? Joy? You're feeling now?"

He cocked his head, the colors tangled on his face. "I do not know if they are emotions, but when I interact with you my tactile sensors are more... excitable."

"You saved my life."

"I was merely following your father's orders."

"Those weren't orders. You *wanted* to save me."

He stood taller, his face muddier. "Wanted?"

Spindle was more than an android assistant. He was artificially intelligent, just like the duplicates. But the Paladins rationalized his existence, said he was closely monitored and encoded to never think freely. That was the difference, they said. Duplicates, they were like viruses, spreading throughout the world for their own purposes. Their number one priority was to survive. *They* were self-centered, not Spindle. He existed to serve us. That, they said, was the difference.

The first time Spindle came to me as the shadow, he followed my father's orders. It was a one-time shot. The Paladins would figure that out, saw my father had set up Spindle to activate my Paladin potential.

The second time he came as the shadow to save us in the Rime, that wasn't so easy. My father knew encrypted orders weren't going to survive after the first time. And he knew they wouldn't destroy Spindle. So he took a chance. He instilled the ability for Spindle to choose. Spindle could've turned into a self-serving duplicate. Maybe he took the chance because Pivot was watching, or maybe my father installed some safety precautions. No idea. Either way, when it came time, Spindle *chose* to override his Paladin-installed programming and save me.

I didn't tell Spindle that. Maybe he already knew. Maybe nobody knew. I saw it all when I absorbed his intelligence long ago, but it didn't make sense until now. I held out my hand and he took it. His was warm and soft. I took it with both hands and shook gently. Really, all I wanted to say was, "Thank you, Spindle."

His face was rosy red, swirling with darker, bubbly shades. "You are quite welcome, Master Socket."

A raccoon stepped into a spider's web. It sat on its haunches and rubbed its face, staring at us with bandit eyes.

"No one comes out here anymore?" I asked.

"It has been quite some time since someone walked this path."

"Pivot's gone," I said. "He's not coming back."

"I am afraid not, Master Socket."

A rogue breeze rushed through the limbs. A band of leaves swirled off the ground and danced overhead. The wind held them high, circling tighter, falling, then rising again. A wave passed through my body, starting at my head and ending in the pit of my stomach, expanding until I felt like I was glowing. I put my hand over my gut and smiled.

"Funny," I said. "I don't know who Pivot is, but I feel like I've known him all my life." Spindle's face was radiant like never before. "You know? Even thinking about him… it fills me."

"He has that effect, I am told."

The leaves pulled together in a tighter, shifting bunch as the wind twisted. Then, all at once, it evaporated and the leaves fluttered down like crinkly snowflakes. I pulled one from my hair. The breeze whipped through the banyan tree, disturbing none of the trees around it. The limbs shook. For a moment, I could see him standing on a branch. Bronze skin. Bleached hair over his eyes.

And then the breeze fell silent. The apparition gone.

"I will miss them," Spindle said.

"Them?"

"Master Pivot, of course." His face darkened. "And the late Master Broak. I will miss them both."

"Your programming skipped a beat, Spindle. You'll miss Broak?"

"Why, yes. He was a promising young man. Very bright. Full of life. The world is a sadder place without him."

"You do know he tried to kill me, right? Twice."

"Yes."

"And you think the world will be sad? Check your logic, Spindle. I'm not sure the world misses him."

"He was a beautiful person. I knew him from the time he was born. I cared for him." The sun reflected on his face, dimmed when a cloud passed over. "He warned us there was something wrong with him, and we did not listen."

"What're you talking about? Broak didn't warn anyone, he fooled us all. He was supposed to start the next generation of Paladins that protected humanity and he turned on us. Where was the warning?"

"He told us all, Master Socket." Spindle tilted his head. *Is it not obvious?* "He told us he was broken."

Broken. He was broke. He was *Broak.*

He changed his own name.

Was he calling out, telling the world he was hurt? That Pike controlled him like a puppet? Someone come save me. I'm broken. Or was the name just a joke, a chance to laugh right in our faces? He didn't want to be human because humans were imperfect. *They* were broken. And since he was human, he was broke. He wanted something better. Something perfect. Until then, he was Broak.

"What was his real name?" I asked.

"Master Vestal was his birth name."

"Well, then, let's pause for the memory of Master Vestal."

Spindle thought for a moment, then brightened. "Yes, I would like that very much."

"Should we pause at the tagghet field?"

"He would like that, Master Socket, but I believe right here and now is appropriate."

We turned to the sunrise. I closed my eyes, felt the warmth on my face. Birds called. Insects buzzed. Dew dripped from the leaves, splattered on the ones below.

Master Vestal. A much better name.

A change in the air pressure. "Are you expecting someone?" I asked.

"Perhaps."

A leaper stopped at the wall. A servy glided out, the eyelight pointed at us. Two people followed. Streeter stopped immediately. His mouth hung open. It was his first time in the Preserve. He didn't notice us down the sloped path under the palms. Chute stepped out of the leaper and didn't see the wondrous jungle. She headed directly for us. I sprinted toward her. We stopped a few feet apart. My chest melted like chocolate, dripping inside. Her freckled complexion was so smooth.

"Are you all right?" I asked.

"Yeah." Her shins, knees to ankles, were wrapped in violet leg warmers. "Circulation enhancers are helping."

"Are they going to be all right?"

"They're fine."

"So they're… they're all right?"

She nodded. Smiled. *Yeah. They're all right.*

248

When I saw her last, her legs had disappeared in the rip, but now she was in front of me. *She's all right.*

The awkward space between us evaporated. We fell forward like we'd been pushing on a wall and now it was suddenly gone. She threw her arms around my neck. I squeezed back, breathing her essence. Satisfying the ache.

"I'm so happy to see you," she whispered.

Energy beamed from my core, enveloped us. Nothing separated us, not even our flesh. Our emotions flowed from one body to the next. I could've held her like that for days.

Streeter's mouth gaped open. "Take it easy until you get a room, why don't you."

Streeter was plump as ever. Clearly he'd found the all-you-can-eat kitchen was no joke. He tried to look disgusted by the hug, but he couldn't stop smiling. He put out his hand but I put him in a headlock. He punched me back, shoved me off the path into the small trees. I fell in the leaves, drenched in dew. He held out his hand and pulled me out.

"Man, I'm glad to see you, Socket." We shook hands a long time, even came close to hugging.

"I want you guys to meet one of my best friends," I said. "This is Spindle."

"Really?" Streeter feigned surprise. "Because we met him a month ago."

"You did?"

"He's been taking care of us. He took us to breakfast, walked us to the infirmary and rode the leapers with us. Can you believe this place?"

Streeter rambled on about servys, holographic imagers and bottomless kitchens. Spindle's face lit up. Streeter, in mid-sentence, held up his hand for a high-five but Spindle buried his fist in it. Streeter shook it.

"You taught them the *stick-it* handshake?" I said to Spindle. He cocked his head, slightly, his face lit up.

"Really? You taught them... I can't believe you taught them—"

"It's cute," Chute said.

"It's not *cute*," Streeter added. "It's just the way he shakes hands. Right, Spindle?"

"Do you know where he got that handshake?" I asked.

"It is my way." Spindle's eyelight blinked. *Don't ruin the moment, Master Socket.*

I looked back and forth between their faces. Streeter waited for my revelation. *Don't ruin it.* "You're right. That's the way they do it," I said.

"This is a new world, Socket," Streeter said. "They do things differently around here."

"You have no idea."

The trees shook and showered us with dew. The leaves fell like autumn arrived. We jumped back to get out of the rain. Hiding in the dark canopies, tiny golden lights blinked at us by the hundreds.

"What is this place?" Chute asked.

"The Preserve is a man-made, enclosed environment supporting the growth of over ten thousand botanical species..."

Spindle spouted the introductory speech. Chute and Streeter scanned the vast jungle. They wouldn't be here long. They would go back home soon. They were normal people; they needed to live normal lives. I wasn't going home. I would stay. I would train. I would become a Paladin. Between us, things would change. Streeter was right: this was the last day for the Watchdogs. It was officially over. But for today, we were still Watchdogs.

The leaves rustled again. A red bat darted out. I held up my hand and Rudder hit it like a rubber toy, curling his long tail through my fingers and nuzzling against me. His essence burst down my arm.

Chute squealed.

250

"This is Rudder." I held my hand out like a small platform. He stood. Bowed.

After introductions and Rudder doing a little show, Chute held her hand flat. He walked onto it and rolled over, twining his tail between her fingers. "He's so soft." She pushed him against her neck and he purred louder.

"Does he bite?" Streeter asked.

"Not that I know of," I said.

Streeter stepped back. Chute dangled him by the tail. "You hold him."

"Don't force him on me, Chute! What's your problem?"

"He's just an innocent creature, Streeter. Like a kitty."

He shook his hands and backed up another step. "Yeah, well, I don't know where that kitty's been. I mean, that thing could have rabies or Ebola. You don't know, Chute."

Rudder's eyes opened wide. *[Ebola?]*

[Never mind him,] I thought back.

"There are a lot more." I pointed to the golden lights. "One of every color."

"Can we see them?" Chute asked.

"Oh, you're going to see them. I'm going to show you everything."

The sun rose above low lying clouds. We shaded our eyes against the glare. A monkey howled. A bobcat cried. Something slithered nearby. We paused in the new morning without a word. The pause just happened, and they didn't even know it. We just stood there. Listening. Seeing. *Being.*

"What's going to happen to you, Socket?" Chute whispered.

"I'm staying here."

"What about us?"

"You're going home."

She hooked her finger around mine. "You're not coming?"

"There're some things to sort out first, but I'll be home to see you. I'd like to see them stop me. Right now, I'm sure there's a test or two they want to run. Right, Spindle?"

Spindle was still pausing. Or maybe he didn't want to get involved. He stared ahead.

Rudder crawled down her arm and wrapped his tail around our hands, squeezing them tighter. Hanging upside down. "Rudder will keep you company," she said. "While I'm gone."

"Yeah. He'll watch out for me."

Chute smiled and shook my hand. Rudder scrambled up my arm and lay on my shoulder, nuzzling against my neck with a deep groan. He sensed Chute's sadness and batted his eyes at her, tried to make her laugh. She just smiled. It was all she could do. I wasn't coming home, at least not yet.

She looked at the sunrise. The light flashed in her eyes. "I went to the Grand Canyon when I was little, but this place... this is beautiful."

"It is quite grand," I said.

"Quite grand?" Streeter scowled. "Are you freaking kidding me? When the hell do you say quite grand?"

"I just... I don't know. It just seemed like the thing to say."

"Quite grand." He waved a stick through the spider web and peeled it to the side, muttering, "He's lost his freaking mind."

"Shall we?" Spindle said, extending his arm. "There is a lot to see and little time."

Around the banyan tree and into the jungle we went. I didn't know what the next day would bring. Or the day after that. I just knew it was a great day. A perfect day.

Just as it is.

The Discovery of Socket Greeny

ABOUT THE AUTHOR

Tony Bertauski lives in Charleston, SC with his charming wife, Heather, and two great kids, Ben and Maddi. He's a teacher at Trident Technical College and a columnist for the Post and Courier. He's published two textbooks on landscape design. He was also a 2008 winner of the SC Fiction Contest for his short story entitled, *4-Letter Words.* You can always find out more at bertauski.com.

Made in the USA
Lexington, KY
16 November 2012